The Girl in the Mirror

Book 3

P. COSTA

THE GIRL IN THE MIRROR BOOK 3

iUniverse books may be ordered through booksellers or by contacting:

iUniverse
1663 Liberty Drive
Bloomington, IN 47403
www.iuniverse.com
844-349-9409

ISBN: 978-1-6632-4534-2 (sc)
ISBN: 978-1-6632-4533-5 (e)

Print information available on the last page.

iUniverse rev. date: 09/29/2022

I would like to dedicate this book to my patient, kind husband, who so graciously did not mind all the hours spent writing, editing or sending the books, and financially supporting me.

And to my Dear friend Barbara who came to my rescue many times.

I am also very grateful for Lucy who kept me going with anticipation.

I did not save Lucy she saved me.

Within a month long after the Olympics were over. Long after the parade in Fresno welcoming April back. They had settled back into their routines with the exception of staring at the medals displayed in a wooden case in the parlor. One was Bronze the other two are Gold. Now April could start to work with the colt again who was half grown.

A production company came to the Di Angelo's home. They were promoting songs by artists, and wanted to know if they could have written permission to use April's ride with the U.S. Olympic Team. This would be on television to promote the song "JUMP" by Van Halen, to earn the team funds. They showed the Di Angelo's a preliminary of the video they made and April loved it.

Within three months after the Olympics, investigators came. They came with a warrant when Gordon was not home. They were rude and pushy and Miranda Di Angelo was not having any of that. Miranda walked into her kitchen and locked the door. She called her husband to come home and asked him to bring some deputies with him.

Gordon Di Angelo was the Sheriff of the town. He was not an aggressive man. But if he was pushed or felt his family threatened, he would not stand by and watch that happen. His deputies brought with them a sense of calm, a witness, and common sense.

As they came into the drive way, Gordon realized these were not police at all. They were private investigators sent by the state. Gordon got out of his cruiser and all four of his deputies joined him. "Good Evening" and Gordon extended his hand to shake theirs. They were not there to be friendly or to shake hands. "I am the Sheriff of this town and these are my deputies Gordon explained. I understand you want to take April Di Angelo with you, without an explanation."

One of the men spoke, "We have a warrant for an arrest for the person or persons who abducted the girl April. She is to be taken back to her biological parents" he said.

"I don't think so" Gordon replied. "You see, six years ago we adopted April and her name is Di Angelo. It is legal and I will show you the paperwork."

Gordon invited he men into his home, while Miranda almost hissed. Gordon was back down stairs in no time to show the men the adoption papers, when they were signed.

Gordon explained, "You can see she arrived over six years ago on a bus. She did not know her last name, she did not know much where she came from, her address, nothing. She came with a small suitcase with old clothing and a stuffed tiger."

"People on the bus took care of her. From our understanding, she was put on a bus to head to California to be with an Aunt. But no one came, no one showed up. In conclusion there was no Aunt."

"April lived like a homeless person in an old car, fending for herself. I also want to say there were over two thousand fliers, on line notices, UPI wires sent looking for her parents. These were sent to law agencies everywhere. It was all legally handled by a law office here in Fresno."

"All during that time we took care of her. No one abducted her. She was never stolen. If at all she left on her own. We have paperwork showing extreme abuse, from X-rays of old- fractures and scars. All of these came from the hospital when we legally adopted her. There is no way a family who hurt her, who abused her should ever have her back." Gordon was in full swing of defending his daughter and their right as parents. "You may have copies of this paperwork, if you contact Judge Du Val at the county courthouse. He will be in tomorrow and his legal secretary's name is Missy" he said.

The men each in turn examined the paperwork that was legal and notarized. There was a legal birth certificate and the Di Angelo's listed as legal parents. They looked at each other and then one said. "We don't know what happened. We do know there is a Mother that her child disappeared and she saw what she believed was her in the Olympics. She was adamant that the rider was her daughter. We had a very difficult time finding you folks and if we could just speak to your daughter, maybe we could clarify this and it would all be over with."

Just then a car pulled up, it was Lauren, April's friend with her Father Daniel. He was also a Congressman from their area. He was to pick up his daughter Lauren and April at the stable and bring April home. Miranda began to feel hot, and went outside.

Miranda motioned to Lauren and April that April should hide and said it in Spanish. April understood, she lay down on the back seat while Daniel pulled the car to the barn. April slipped out of the back seat door, crouched down, went to the barn, bridled

Dobbins and rode out the back gate. April rode Dobbins across the meadow up over the hills and if she had to, she would stay outside all night long.

April thought while she was out, she would ride to the farms and feed the calves. During this time, Congressman Daniel came onto the porch with Lauren and spoke calmly with Miranda. "So, Lauren finished her lesson and was wondering when April was coming home?" he said winking at Miranda.

"Well, I don't know Miranda said, you know how she is, it is hard to get her off of the back of a horse" and they both laughed.

The men in the house came out when they heard April's name. "Is she here for us to talk to?" they asked.

"Oh no, we just stopped here to let Miranda know Lauren finished her lesson. She wanted to thank her, as April was the one who referred us to the trainers."

"April was still at the center when we left."

"Oh, may we have that address?" the investigator asked.

Gordon Di Angelo stepped outside, "No you may not have that address. April is a minor. No one is going to speak to her unless we are present. Now I have to admit you are getting on my bad side here. I already gave you information you will need and it is available tomorrow."

The investigators stepped off of the Di Angelo's porch and headed to their cars. No words were exchanged they simply backed out of the drive way and left

Gordon stood there with his deputies and told them to take the squad car and follow those fools. He wanted to know where they were going. Never in his life had Gordon been so upset, and now, where was his daughter?

Gordon realized April had come home with Daniel who the Congressman of their Congressional area. He asked Daniel, "What can I do about this? Do they have the right to come in be pushy and go threaten my wife?"

Congressman Daniel said "No, they do not have that right, they should have sent a certified letter. They were trying to show their weight or muscle, Daniel said. And that was very wrong. I am going to contact the Congressman and the Senator from the east, as this was clearly abuse of excessive power."

Gordon thanked him and said he wanted to go out and find his daughter. Gordon shook hands with Congressman Daniel and went to the barn. He noticed Dobbins was gone and he guessed where April would be. Gordon saddled his mare and followed Dobbins tracks.

~~≈≈~~

April was pitching hay to the calves from up on top of the barn when Gordon arrived at the barn.

"Hey you up there" he called to his daughter.

"Hey you, back at cha" April said smiling.

Gordon dismounted and went to help his daughter. April was almost finished, so they sat on a bale and talked.

"Dad, what happened tonight" she asked her father.

"It seems there is someone looking for you darlin'. She claims to be your real Mother and wants you to come back home."

April sat there for a minute to think. Try as she might she could not recall that life anymore, not like she used to. Her life was happy and full, she felt safe. Deep inside her, April felt sorry for the Mother from her past. She did not remember being treated badly by her. She remembered her being busy, but always trying to protect her. April could not for all she was, dis-like or hate this woman.

April put herself in the woman situation and said, "I can imagine if it were me, I would want to know too" she said to her Dad. "I don't remember like I used to, but I don't think she ever did anything to hurt me. I feel sorry for her in a way you know what I mean Dad?"

"Yes, I do" he said. "April you are a good person, with a good heart, you always put others feelings before yours. Just take it slow, and let things play out, don't push, ok?" he asked his daughter.

April stood up and hugged her Dad and she began to feel very emotional. April pulled back and looked at her Dad directly into his face. "Dad, I want to thank you for taking me in, giving me a chance. I don't know where I would be or what would have happened to me if you and Mom did not reach out to me." April had to take a breath, "I know there is a kind loving Father in Heaven who watched over me. I also know nothing just happens. There is always reason for it all. So how ever I did get out here, there was a reason. That's why I truly feel I am here with you and Mom."

"There is no hate in my heart Dad. I have to let go and trust God's plan and see where this goes. She may be my birth Mother and I do owe that much to her. But you and Mom are my parents." The two of them hugged each other. There would never be any incident or event that would break this bond.

"Come on, Mom's probably wringing her hands by now" Gordon said. The two of them climbed back down the loft ladder. Mounted and left for home. When they got there Miranda walked to the barn to speak to them.

"Are you two alright?" she asked. "Yes Mam we are" April said jokingly. April was finished before her Dad as she only had a bridle to take off Dobbins. April put Dobbins out in the pasture and then she ran to her Mother hugging her.

April looked up at her Mom and said, "I love you Mom, this will all work out for the good, you watch and see" squeezing her ever harder.

As time went on, there was a hearing that no one had to be at. Two Judges appointed for both sides reviewed the paperwork, and decided there was no case, there was no cause to return this girl. What the Di Angelo's did was prudent and legal. They were concerned for a little girl living in the street. They did nothing wrong, and April did have the final say. April said what she felt. The Di Angelo's were her parents, legal or otherwise. It did not end there. After conversations with her parents and an interview with her Bishop, April sat down several times over the following weeks to write a letter.

April wanted it right she wanted to express her gratitude, to let the birth Mother to know April was happy. April would sit there for an hour or more deciding what to say, write it down only to scribble it out.

Dear Birth Mother,

I wanted to sit down and write you a letter to thank you. Thank you for giving me birth. I cannot imagine giving birth, caring for that child and have it disappear. For that I humbly apologize, but I myself do not know what happened.

I am sure that when I "disappeared" you were at a great loss. But I assure you I was always in the care of a kind Heavenly Father. He led me to the best people who watched over me. Then he brought me to a place where I have been treated with love and care, I am happy. I I am glad you recognized me in the Olympics it proves that you never gave up hope. Hope is a good thing, an eternal blessing.

Please know that I feel I owe a great debt to you for my life. But my parents are the ones who are raising me. I owe so much to them as well. I have no hate in my heart towards you, only love. I don't know who I would be with you, or how I would have turned out. I want you to know I am doing well. I raise calves, and give pony rides. I do well in school, and I go to church every Sunday. I have many friends, and my parents are good, kind and strict with me. I love them very much.

Please know that one day we shall meet, get to know one another other all about each other. I feel it is destined to happen, although I don't know how. But when we do, we will be blood relatives that greet each other with love and respect.

I will trust God and let him handle this. Know that, I mean this will every beat of my heart. Again, I am grateful for all you have done

for me and hope you forgive me. With love, April
Di Angelo

April finished the letter, folded it and handed it to her Mother. April did not know where to send it anyway. Miranda put the letter on a pile on her desk where all the papers from the attorney were.

Later that day she dug and found the attorney's address to their law office. That was the only address she had. Miranda addressed the envelope but before she put April's letter inside, she read her daughters letter. Miranda was filled with compassion. She felt her daughter did a good job expressing herself, Miranda felt she also should write a note to the birth Mother, and she did.

Dear Birth Mother,

I want you to know that your daughter is a joy and a blessing to us, as we were not blessed with any children of our own. I would like to have a correspondence with you, to keep you informed about April. We too are grateful to you for your unknowing sacrifice and know it was not in vain. Your daughter is a blessing to many people and in time you will get to know her, I promise. Thank you sincerely, Miranda Di Angelo

The letters were sent and received and the birth Mother was overjoyed for she knew the truth. April would never have blossomed under their roof. But now she could. Now she would

get to know her daughter in the best of circumstances. How great, how kind God truly is, she thought.

And throughout the years, April and Miranda kept their promise, they did write, often. The Mother replied when she could, her life would take many turns and twists, those letters were always a source of comfort to her.

Her other children were at times troubled, most were grown and gone. Still some came home for money and to ask for her car because they wrecked theirs. The last two boys at home were good boy's they worked hard on the farm. She had hoped they would stay and work it out with their Dad. The one wanted to go to the Navy but the other liked tractors and machinery, so she felt if one stayed so would the other, they were that close.

Her husband became sour over the years, almost bitter. He had crazy ideas and if she just remained silent, it would pass. She loved this man for the man he was, but anymore she did not know him. They had grown apart. Through the years he did not spend much time with her. They never went out to eat, or visited anyone, or attend church together. They did not argue much, but they did not talk much either.

She knew that if they had stayed active in church that would have helped. A date once a week, or even once a month would have made a difference as well.

Married couples should never take their relationship as partners for granted, or guess that person will never stray. Marriage takes work. Helping each other, doing for one another, never one sided. Married partners are a team, working for the one goal they have in mind. Sacrifice is often present and can be uncomfortable, but if you pray together, work together, you will overcome remain a strong couple.

The idea of marriage counseling crossed the Mother's mind many times, but she knew her stubborn husband would not go. She decided that she would go, and see what the counselor could offer her to enhance the marriage even if "he" was unwilling.

It was a huge task, but one she wanted to try. She was not one to throw away a relationship for personal reasons. They made a pact before God years ago, and from time to time it was important they seek help. Either from people who loved them or a counselor, either way, help is there if you want it.

Our Plan

APRIL WAS HOME, SHE LONGED TO BE THERE THE ENTIRE TIME SHE was in Germany. April felt she had missed out on so much. She was in love the man of her dreams. He had four long legs, and was red as the setting sun. He always looked for her and would whinny when he saw her.

April spent many hours with him, brushing him, making him shine and talking to him. She spoke softly to him and he responded with funny sounds or tilting his head. Sometimes he would dance around her. Yes, these two were quite a pair. They were seen walking together, riding in town, racing across fields, just like a couple and she was often teased about it.

Native Son was ready for professional training and it took a few months to find the right man. He did not look the part. He was a mess from head to toe, not dirty but untidy. He was an older man, one who had lived at the tracks as a young man. He had success, but not the kind he yearned for. So, here he was looking at a stallion with very impressive papers.

Native Son as she called him was truly from great blood lines and he had potential, he was built to run. Marty was a humble man, one who did not say much unless it needed to be said. Marty was a horse man thru and through, he lived and breathed horses.

April learned much from Marty, she insisted she was going to ride Native Son and that was fine for now. This colt needed conditioning, he behaved for April so why not? This was the green light April had hoped for, to ride Native Son whenever and where ever she wanted.

They were seen crossing fields and woods from the highway. And when they rode into town, it was usually racing someone's truck. Yes, conditioning was a blast. April enjoyed it very much as did Native Son. His ears up forward and his eyes ahead, as if he were looking for adventure.

They entered some B races, and he won twenty four of them with no losses. Marty told the Di Angelo's their horse was better than that, he was racing scrap. It was time to put him in good races so they did. Native Son raced in California and Mexico and there was not a horse that could keep pace with him, the earnings were good.

April committed to return ten percent of what they won, back to the track where they raced to make racing better. To open it up to anyone who had a good horse to race, not only for the wealthy. Then she paid ten percent tithing to her church.

To April, money never held much value, the land did. A lot of land that provided fertile crops did. April became tenacious about saving money. Each race won would purchase a farm. Those farms were sought out by Arthur, their accountant April had hired. Sometimes she was privileged to go along to see them but other times it was Arthur's expertise and choice. If he had questions, he turned to the Agricultural centers for maps to check out the land.

Over time it would be one farm and then maybe another in that same county or next to it. Time after time, either they were for sale or Arthur would approach them and ask himself. The worst they could say was no. Often more than no, he heard yes.

It gave relief to the owners of the farms. They were paid a more than fair value and were allowed to continue to live on the farm. As they always had, with no expense to them. They were asked about the fields. Their opinions often, as it was good to stay active and be involved.

As the racing money came in it was used to buy farms, all across America. One by one, state by state. Some were bought in groups to accumulate fertile lands. The former owners could stay if they chose to and live there, until final plans were made. No one knew except April, her accountant and the sellers.

At many of those races it was not uncommon for April to find someone down on their luck. Like the time the young fellow was sitting on his tailgate. April intuitively asked him what was wrong. He told her he had world class hounds that could track anything. But he did not have enough money to get started in a business. April asked him how much that would take. He thought and scribbled and decided about seven thousand, with kennels, and trucks, advertising, and so on. April wrote a number down and told the man to call the number and give him this name, it was a pass code. He looked at April shocked

"You mean you will help me?" he asked her.

"Why wouldn't I" she replied, "They sure sound special and who knows, maybe one day I will be in need of a good tracking bloodhound" and they laughed.

The number to call was to Author. A man they hired from Fresno. He had worked at the shoe factory for years, living on pennies. He was a great numbers man working numbers in his head was easy for him. That was April's accountant. As the winnings came in from the races it was not uncommon for someone to call for Author to authorize release of funds to them.

Arthur would always listen but prior to releasing funds, he would visit the person with the need before the funds were distributed. He was sort of the watchdog over the money and if there was fraud he notified the Di Angelo family.

Yes, you could count on Arthur, who was grateful to be out of the factory. He made more than enough money to support his family. He had one son, who was a lot like Arthur. Cole was a great kid, mature, kind, very respectful and he loved his parents. Arthur's wife was sickly, she did not travel. She was on oxygen at home and it was a relief to have the medical necessities she needed. The Di Angelo family made sure his wife was well taken care of.

And April, well Arthur thought of her as if he were her Uncle. April was a pip, a really kind person. April was always helping someone, but she was the one paying as she helped. There were many of them some were at the spur of the moment.

~~~

Like the time when April was walking on a side street and noticed signs to raise money to pay for a senior center. April saw people doing laps in the pool for money. She asked a woman at the counter for her help.

She told the woman to call all the radio stations and TV station and let them know April Di Angelo was there to raise money and putting out a challenge to match funds.

The woman knew who April was, almost everyone did. This girl was the one who rode the fastest horse on the track she had ever witnessed. She had also been in the Olympics and was a Champion. The women bought hot dogs, rolls, and lots of ice tea and lemon aide, and made the calls.

Meanwhile with a borrowed swim suit April was in the pool doing laps. In no time a TV crew showed up and in a half hour the place was packed. Someone put a rope around the pool area so they would let April alone. Swimmers could come in, but no one else.

Lap after lap, each time she made five dollars, April was an avid swimmer and she was determined to stick this out. There was an elderly man sitting on a bench watching her swim, and she planned to swim until that man got up and walked away.

After an hour the man was still there and April was beginning to show fatigue. The senior center was packed, kids were bringing in money they earned mowing lawns. Car dealerships were contributing and shouting out challenges to their competitors for matching funds and all this time April kept swimming.

April tried to push away the ache in her arms and legs, she thought if that old man can sit there watching me that long, I can swim longer. And April pushed on. As money came in, a woman would fill in a cardboard gage with a red marker they were over half of their goal.

Still April swam on, lap after lap. The crowd inside swelled. There was very little room to move and the street outside was just as crowded. Camera crews all wanted to talk to April but instead they did interview other people that were there. Every once in a while a celebrity would pop in and give their support, and the people loved it.

April kept swimming and as she made another pass she saw the red on the goal up to eighty eight percent, she sighed inside and pushed herself to keep going.

There was a flurry of people in and out, money was flowing in and at long last the red filled to the top of the gage. They had more than met their quota. But still that old man was sitting there and April had promised herself not to stop unless he stopped watching her.

As it turned out the elderly man had been sleeping with his eyes open. He never watched April swim, but he was able to convince April to keep going. As she exited the pool, she was exhausted. Some rushed to her with towels and she gratefully accepted them. Soon April was dressed and out in the street. No one recognized her. She walked out the back door down to the track to find her parents.

The next day the headline in their local paper was "Rider swims to free Senior Center" and there was a picture of a girl swimming. April's Mother questioned April about it and April said she did not know any- thing about it.

April felt she could do laps and help them, and it was a good idea. There were others she had helped, many others.

All that she did was to further glorify God, not her. That was April's nature to follow through to get things done.

That year the Di Angelo's bought the local Radio station. The radio station was bought on a whim by April when she saw only one person working. He was playing modern music when most people that area loved country music. The Radio station quickly became Miranda's pet. She did much good there and became quite proficient operating the equipment.

The women in the community loved old music, gospel songs. And they loved recipes and so that is what the station became in the mornings. By afternoon there were topics of town discussion, and up beat songs. By evening there was news of the day, job openings, and music. The station became Miranda's pet project. Thru this medium she was able to do much good. The station became a meeting place for pets to have their vaccinations at much less cost and bicycle safety for young children. The deputies would inspect their bicycles and teach safe riding.

Miranda's radio station had soldier leaving or returning home. That station parking lot had many activities there, much loved by the community.

"Mr. O' Toole

NATIVE SON WAS GROWING LIKE A WEED, THROUGHOUT THAT year. April would loosen the ponies and they would follow Native Sun as they rode across meadow and thru the forest. On one occasion Mr. O'Toole was visiting his daughter Mrs. Marshall. As he was walking across the meadow, he heard a rumbling sound, something was coming.

There was an old wooden rotting hay wagon in the meadow and he ducked down under it. The many ponies passed by him and all at once he saw her coming hard on the big red. The two jumped right over that wagon. He was impressed. Blimey he just had to get to know that girl better.

So Mr. O'Toole called Judge Du Val's office and requested charges. Now both of them knew this was a game. Maybe cruel but the Judge also felt that April should be reined in a bit. The letter arrived addressed to April. Miranda out of respect did not open it. She waited for her daughter to come home.

When April got home she read the court letter and handed it to her Dad. Gordon quickly realized this was not a court order or a charge. Gordon assumed that Mr. O'Toole was up to something. Gordon was not concerned he knew that Judge Du Val always had April's best interest at heart. If this had been something to be worried about, the Judge would have called him before the letter was sent. The letter asked for April to contact Mr. O'Toole at her earliest convenience. At the bottom was a hand penned note by the Judge, "When you decide to go, let me know in advance, I'd love to go with you."

In a day or two April put in a call to Mrs. Marshall, who was surprised! April explained why she was calling and was then given a day. Mr. O'Toole did not have a telephone in the cabin where he was living. Then April called the court house and spoke with Missy, giving her the date of the meeting, to pass it on to the Judge.

The week passed and on the appointed day, Judge Du Val was in the drive way with his pick-up truck waiting to take April along to Mr. O'Toole's cabin. April washed her face and combed her hair. She was good to go and hopped in the pick-up truck. They greeted one another with a hug and soon the truck was headed to Mr. O'Toole's. "So what did you do to him" the Judge asked April.

April shrugged her shoulders, she did not know, she had not even seen the man.

"Well, we will find out soon enough" the Judge said smiling. The Judge parked his truck near the cabin beside the old man's Willie's Jeep.

The two of them walked to the cabin door and knocked, "Come in" they heard from inside. They entered to find a neat but plainly decorated cabin. There was a round table in the kitchen, set with bowls of soup.

"Come in and sit down, I was about to have lunch so you may as well join me" O'Toole said.

April asked to wash her hands and he led her to the sink and gave her a towel. Then they sat down, and as the potato soup was ladled into the bowels, each man picked up their spoon. April made a loud "Ahem" sound. As they looked at her, April bowed her head to pray aloud.

The old man winked at the Judge and promptly the two of them bowed their heads for the lunch time prayer.

At "Amen" they began to have lunch and the conversation.

"So, the old man said, "You got a summons in the mail from me, did ya?"

"Yes I did Sir, and I am wondering what I did that offended you?" April asked.

"Offend me?" "No, you did not offend me, you were reckless!" he said. reckless?" she restated.

"Absolutely, You almost killed me last week with your horses running amuck across the meadows and through the fields."

April said, "I did not see you, I usually ride this way with the group." "You didn't see me because I was run under that old rickety wagon. Thank Jesus it was there, it saved me life" he said. You came wild like, soaring over the wagon and then you were gone." Mr. O'Toole said.

April saw how excited he was and said, "Seems like you liked it, just the sort of thing to make your blood flow faster" and she smiled.

"Ohh, I'm tellin' ya' this one's a smart one, eh Judge, all wily and tricky!

"That she is sometimes, but I think in this situation she was just letting the ponies run and having fun. I don't believe she saw you at all and never meant you any harm, did you April?" the Judge asked her.

"No Sir, I did not see him or meant anyone any harm, I guess I can't let the ponies run anymore" she said.

"Oh no, don't let me stop you now" he said.

"Tis a fine thing to see a young lass handle all those ponies so well. It truly is a sight to see all those colors in the meadow, beautiful I tell you, just beautiful" Mr. O'Toole said.

Now April was a bit confused, if he liked it, why was he pressing charges? She asked him just that!

"Well, me mind got the best of me, and to be a tellin' you the truth, I just be wantin' to get to know ye a bit better." "But Lass, ye should let a feller know when you plan on running him thru so's he's not murdered while on his walk" he said.

As the conversation went, they all realized how innocent this was, that this girl did not realize people walked that meadow. In the three years of riding there, April never saw one single person. That is why she took the liberty of letting all the ponies run and let them follow Native Son.

All was forgiven and the old man made a date of sorts with April. He wanted her to come and visit him off and on during the summer.

Not for long, just a few minutes here, and a few minutes there. When they left they all shook hands, and Mr. O'Toole kissed the back of April's hand.

The next time she let the ponies run, she made sure she swung by his cabin. When April and Native Son stopped all of the ponies stopped. They loved to eat grass whenever they could. April would holler out "Hello" and if he was in, he would come out on the porch and they would sit awhile, like old friends in the rocking chairs.

He would ask her what her plans were for the day, or if there was something planned for her during the week. They talked a bit more and then April would say good bye, mount and be gone.

He would stand up and watch them all go, he watched until the last speck of color was gone.

On that same day of visiting with Mr. O'Toole, when April got home with the Judge her Dad was there and he wanted to talk with the Judge.

Eddie The Swindler

A CERTIFIED LETTER HAD COME FROM AN EDDIE BARROW, CLAIMING that the mare and colt April bought years ago was stolen. The letter stated she knowingly took advantage of him.

The Judge said for Gordon to see if there was a police report and follow up on that end and when he had that information to drop it off at the courthouse. He would look into it for him. Gordon did all of that next week, along with the bill of sale that was in April's name.

In the months to follow Eddie scheduled court hearing after court hearing insisting that the colt was his. Each time he was turned down. Eddie wanted winning money from the races, at the very least a percentage. And he just kept it up, losing thousands of dollars to attorney's fees and court hearings, which he lost.

April was irritated at his insistence to this futile, ridiculous claim. April asked the Judge Du Val if she offered Eddie two thousand dollars maybe he would sign off and that would be that. The Judge had a paper drawn up, and traveled personally to Eddie's home. He offered the proposal of cash, and when Eddie saw the cash.

Not a check, Eddie signed readily.

So far as the Judge was concerned this was not necessary, but now that Eddie signed off for a second time, this was it! He may complain forever, but this deal was done.

Native Son

It was in the nick of time too, as Native Son was about to enter his first big race in the month of May. Oh he was fast all right. His big problem was if he saw April he would slow down or he would stop.

As difficult as it was for April to accept she agreed to another rider, other than herself. She felt deep inside her, down in the depths of her soul a hurt she could not describe. It came out in tears. April loved her horse, more than most people. She knew the deep love she had for him and it hurt her to not be there, on him when he crossed that finish line.

April could not say much to Marty, his job was to see that Native Son crossed the finish line first. He was a good man, who cared deeply for the horse. But riders had to meet his criteria. He felt April was too small, not experienced enough to race in a big important race like this.

Native Son however had made up his mind. He did school well for the rider Marty chose. But he would not open up, he refused. Marty was not one for whipping a horse, but said if he kept refusing he would bring out a crop. April was furious! April had an awful temper when someone hurt an animal for their own benefit. Truth was all you had to do is "show" Native Son the stick, not hit him.

That evening April wrapped Native Sons feet and legs, she went to a pay phone to call her Dad, and then the hauler who was on the race track grounds. He came with the box truck and April began to lead Native Son out of his assigned stall.

Marty came running towards her asking, "What do you are doing?" he said. "Taking my horse home" was all she said. Marty knew he had crossed a line with April

Marty stood in front of the boarding gate stopping her. "Look I am sorry, but your horse has got to run and he has to open up and find his potential. I felt that you would not be capable or able to move him the way I need, and I see I was wrong."

"No rider can move Native Son as you can. I don't know if the race track will give me hell for putting you on him, but so far as I am concerned you are on for the race." And he walked away to the office of the track.

April rubbed her horses head, "Come on boy, we are going to show them what we are made of." He nickered to her as though he understood. Back in his stall, his groom Byron came over to talk to them both. "You all will do well, I know it. I see the sadness in our boy's eyes. Each time he comes in off of the breeze track. It's you he wants, we's all see it. So when you ride, he will win, I know it, I feel it."

That night April slept in Native Son's stall, she had done that many, many times in his past. She wanted him to know they were one. They were all each other had. Native Son got it, big time! April was like Native Son's Mom. His teacher and his fun, He lived to please her. A mere whisper from her and he listened. She may be young but not any bigger or smaller than the jockeys, and she was his.

If anyone had the right to choose who rode him, it would be her, but for sure make no doubt about it, Native Son chose.

Race Day!

THE NEXT DAY THERE WAS ACTIVITY ALL AROUND THEM APRIL had awoke early, putting her arms around her boy, reassuring him. He nickered to her and soon the groom Byron was there with Native Son's breakfast. April was hungry and had a biscuit with an egg inside. April decided to walk the track. It was early, she had plenty of time before she had to weigh in or dress.

April came back to weigh in with her clothing. April entered her locker area and pulled out her race uniform, her colors were red and yellow, like the sun. She strode to the weigh area and many of the jockeys looked at and talked about her.

April had no intention to be rude even if they were, so she said, "Guys, I am here to race today just like you all are. May God watch over all of us. Keep us and the horses safe. May we all ride fair and hard, and at the finish line may we all be friends." Many nodded their head, and looked at her differently.

There were no problems and soon she was dressed and ready to ride. April waited for Marty to come to her. He would preview how he saw the race. He'd tell her who to watch for, the conditions of the track and give her his best advice how to run the race. Ultimately she would be out there and have to make all the decisions in two or three minutes and then it would all be over.

April could not wait for her boy, she was so excited but calm and soon she saw him all tacked up with his bright yellow around his eyes and red on his face.

Native Son was striking in those colors. When he saw her, his head went up and he whinnied in a greeting. They were here not to play but to win.

This was the Kentucky Derby, for a million dollar purse. The track was one and a half mile long and always on the first Saturday in May. This was in Louisville Kentucky and the first race for the Triple Crown. Native Son was unknown, but not for long. He would keep his name as Native Son and if any one questioned his qualifications in breeding, then and only then would they show their papers.

There were banners, colored streamers, women wearing big crazy hats, in beautiful dresses. Men wore suits, and some with top hats. The crowds were coming in, the grand stands were full. April's Dad was there with a program in hand. Gordon greeted his daughter with a kiss on her forehead. That did not go unnoticed by many of the grooms and jockeys. April did not care she loved her Dad and needed and appreciated his support.

"Are you ready to fly" he jokingly teased her, April just nodded. Soon Marty was there greeting her Father and explaining a lot. Some of the jockeys were mounting and April needed a lift so her Dad helped her, making sure her feet were in the stirrups right.

Marty said, "Don't be afraid, do not be intimidated in the stocks starting gate, he will feel your jitters and be off. Pretend you are both heading out on the breeze track it's no different, but he will trust you. You are at the helm, let him run as he wants, stay with the crowd and at the second turn let him go. See how he feels tight or loose, and then encourage him on.

He can take it he is in pristine shape conditioned to run this track." And that was it.

In no time they were walking down the alley way, the crowd was loud thankfully Native Son was used to things like this from town riding and in the parades and previous races. As they came thru the galley way, April rubbed his neck and told him they were going to have fun. Native Son responded lifting his ears. He was not nervous. Native Son was looking all around. When they settled into the starting gate, he would change his attitude to all work.

The walk to the startup gate was quick. They had the seventh spot in the lineup. Completely unknown, a wild card.

Native Son walked easily into his spot, no rearing and no bad attitude like some of the other horses around them. He was used to the stocks from the beginning of his life and B races.

That was it, they were all in place. April adjusted her tear shield on her visor glasses, and held her hands tight on the reins and waited. She crouched forward, grabbing some of his mane hair and re adjusting the reins. April sat there anticipating the buzzer and opening of the shoot. It all happened so fast, the shoots opened fast and they both came out like a bullet.

Native son was in the outside near the middle of the pack. He kept his pace easily giving April time to see those who Manny told her about. April decided to stay clear of them not wanting to be elbowing or having the horses step on each other.

April knew Native Son's potential. She was not sure about two of the other horses out there, who were now in second and third spot. But she felt she would let Native Son out after that second turn, and she did.

Racing is unique! It feels like a lifetime up in that saddle, when in fact it's a two minute ride. All during the race there is jostling of horses for placement. You hear sound of horse hooves pounding the track and dirt flying into your face throughout the race. All during that time the Jockeys have to pay attention for open spots they can maneuver their ride into for better placement. The sound is very loud, just once it would be an experience at a track so you could understand.

Native Son easily picked up speed rounding the second turn, and he never slowed down. At the half turn he was even with them. At the third turn he was four lengths ahead of them. At the end of the race Native Son won with six lengths ahead of the pack of riders, he breezed across that finish line all alone.

What a surprising finish, reporters came running down the field. The crowds were loud. Whoever bet on Native Son won the odds of 35 to 1. They would all go home with a lot of money in their pockets. Yes, he had proven himself that day. He stood there with flower spray around his neck, his girl on his back, and the Dad, Marty and groom at his left face side, and Mom was on the right. April's parents were beside her. All though out that race Miranda was wringing her handkerchief, it looked like a twisted colorful rag.

Miranda had happy tears and looked at her daughter sitting there on that big horse, with mud streaked face, and looking so much older. She knew that this would open the door wide for April and Native Son, there was no turning back now.

Native Son had no reason to be fearful, he loved to run. Although he did not understand all the whoopla around him, he knew he did something good, and he loved attention.

Marty was so happy he smiled more than April had ever seen. He had his hand on April's boot and her Dad was on the back side of Marty holding onto April's leg. The groom Byron was at Native Sons head, all teeth, he could not stop grinning. He was telling Native Son he was a good boy. Everyone wanted to know who this horse was, how this upset happened.

Marty explained there was no upset. Just a great horse that wanted to prove himself on the track, it happens. With flash bulbs going off from all directions, the reporters were excited to know as much as they could about the horse, rider and owners.

As they walked to the stable areas off of the track, there were people running alongside of them at the rail cheering them on. They were a mix of young people and children. April stopped her horse and asked them to give her their program and she signed their programs.

They were at the stables and April dismounted with some help from her Dad, The groom, Byron untacked Native Son and began washing him down.

And Byron noticed a group of jockeys heading their way. April did not notice as she was talking with her Dad so Byron whistled and said, "Head's up ya all" and then Dad noticed the group of jockeys heading their way.

They stood before April some could not speak English, but to April that was ok, she understood Spanish. April's Mother had taught her to speak it. Some shook her hand, and some bumped her shoulder said "great race". April thought this was so decent of these guys and she thanked each of them. They did not have to come. Not all of them were there, some did not agree with her racing on the track.

The winnings sealed many things for April, she and Arthur began to work the farms already purchased into a company. They both had brain storms what it should be called. They came up with two names. "Friendly Farms or D Farms" April liked the first choice, but learned there was already a company with that name, so they went with D Farms.

Now this was sealed. April would continue to have D Farm business. And it would help many others. Last year she began with Mrs. Adams farm. She offered her a fair price and bought the entire farm, lock stock and barrel. April bought and brought 150 milking cows to that barn. Just as they had other farms purchased.

It all seemed so easy to many, April was a winner how glamorous it all was. The truth was April suffered with a condition her Dr. struggled to understand.

Her hands would peal, for no reason. They would itch, the skin turned red on her hands and the outer skin would become hard, dead, and would peel. April had to take a steroid to keep her skin appear normal, she had to monitor the meds. Sometimes a whole pill if the condition was bad, or half if just a tad annoying, other times she took nothing.

April had to monitor this all the time. No one knew but her parents, and that is how she wanted it to be.

April spoke with Mrs. Adam's grandson, and offered him job milking. Now Brock was an interesting character, he was usually in trouble in school and at home. Brock was fifteen now. Two years older than April. Brock was mouthy and belligerent. He wanted out from his home life. So April offered him a job that,

"If" he agreed to obey the rules. He would live in the house, on other half from his Grandma.

All April was asking of Brock was to milk the cows in the morning. April would milk nights. It was not hard work, but he had to pay attention. Then he let the cows in the pasture at the feed lot, and put out the feed April mixed the night before. There would be other jobs, but nothing difficult. But before she would help him, he had to sign an agreement paper. If he did not keep his end of the bargain, he would be out of the house in the street. April would not tolerate slacking.

Brock jumped at the chance. He had older friends move his stereo, clothing, guitar, and things into the one half of the home. Brock was strictly forbidden to play the guitar or loud music in the home, he had to play in the garage.

Mrs. Adams did not like loud music and she should not have to put up with it. He absolutely had to be more respectful to his Grandmother. To stop ignoring her and have a conversation with her once in a while, act decent!

So it began Brock did milk every morning and put the feed out and let the cows in the meadow so they could graze and eat at the feed lot.

After school April would get off of the bus at Mr. Adams and she would drive the cows into the barn, and tie them. Then she would milk the cows. Then when finished put the milking canisters and milking machines in a tub to be washed and sterilized.

April would mix a batch of feed and let it sit. Then the cows were then bedded down with fresh straw from the straw chopper. Then she was done. April would walk the distance home, it cleared her mind. Sometimes her Mom would ride their four-wheeler to the farm and let it there for April to ride home. At home April fed the ponies, and sometimes went for a ride on her guy and wish school was out, so she had more time.

April continued the pony rides on weekends only. There was a new crop of kids. Those "kids" her age were now in sports or had hobbies of their own. Many of them did not to ride anymore. The new kids always had an excitement and joy to ride, that April enjoyed being around that.

Two rides on Saturday, that was it, she rode Native Son. When all the kids were gone, April rode her boy until evening when it was her turn to milk. The milk prices were fairly good.

A milk check came every two weeks, and Brock got paid the next day after Miranda went to the bank.

In less than two months there were pilot barns like April had set up with Brock.

But on the D farms, the owners if they chose to stay were the surrogate parents to the kids who wanted to live there to work or go to college. They lived on the farm, it was their home. They commuted to college and milking paid their tuition and they had some spending money.

The meals at home were free, as was their lodging and clothing. There was no cost to them, and they were well paid.

All of the milk checks came to Arthur. He deposited them and then he would figure time sheets for milking and who did what. And all of the tuitions were paid by Arthur. There was a catch, they had to have passing grades and attend church.

Over time many students became advocates for D Farms, telling everyone how good the company was to them. They worked and their tuition was paid and they had some spending money. It was a way for them to go to college and not be burdened with a huge dept at the end of their education. They were not allowed "partying" unless it was a holiday. They lived like a family, all problems were worked out. Some failed they did not want any "instructions" to their life. Others were grateful.

All across the west into the mid sections, across the south and pushing into the east there were fifty five D Farms operating this way.

Field work was done by custom farmers, who were always looking for work. They all signed contracts with D. Farms.

Once a year, one good sized steer was butchered for use for those who lived and worked on D. farms. Everyone was well taken care of. There were chickens raised for food and chickens for eggs. Two or three hogs raised, two for each farm and one to donate, fish in the ponds.

The farm provided most of what they needed. Monies were allotted for other expenses electric, heat, groceries, or any repairs any large expense had to be approved and paid by Arthur.

The success rate of the college kids was phenomenal. The college kids only had good to say about D farms. They had employment every day, with two days a week off. They were committed to staying and enjoyed the home living situation. Every one helped where they could. Many of them graduated with no debt, thanks to D farms. This was all set in motion long before Native Son's race that would be a whirl wind leaving April so little time.

Now if only Brock could get with it, after a year, he became restless. Brock had put a truck together in his spare time and was driving all around town. Especially at night not coming in till three a.m. and too tired to get up to milk. April had it with Brock, Brock was sixteen and she and Brock had words. Loud, clear to the point words. He decided he had enough as well, so she kicked him out.

Brock's things went sailing out of the bedroom window, everything including his sheets. Worse of all, he was ignorant and rude to his Grandmother who sat crying most days.

Now April would get up at four a.m. go to the Adams farm and milk the cows. That took two and half hours. Then she put them out, another half hour, which it was now seven a.m. April had to wash and get to school, sometimes she was late. If a cow had a calf, or if a heifer was stubborn to milk. April also had to go back after school and put the cows back in, a half hour, milk them, two and a half hours, and bed and straw and feed them. Three and half hours, then go home and feed the ponies and spend some time with Native Son. Often it was after dark when she got into the house. It was not uncommon for her to fall asleep at the dinner table.

Her Dad was angry, this was not what he wanted for his daughter, but he said nothing. He helped where he could. The steers kept him busy, as April kept taking them in. Now with the milk cows there were bull calves and heifers born all year round. On one evening Dad and Mom took April to an outdoor trip, for ice cream or a burger. While they were there Brock pulled up in his truck revving the engine, he was a full blown bad boy motor head.

Dad opened his door and said, "I'll be right back." Miranda pulled at his shirt to stop him but both she and April knew there was no point he would say what he wanted to say to Brock who needed his butt kicked. There was no argument, but words were loud at times. Brock's hands were flying in the air, and soon Gordon walked back to his truck. "He is whining you gypped him" he said with a half laugh.

"He was willing to work, but you were killing him."

"Oh I'd like to kill him" April said. "That's the thanks you get for helping someone. I learned my lesson. I don't believe you can change someone who has a bad attitude and he sure has one. Let him live in his truck. His parents don't want him back and I refuse to let him free load off his Grandmother. He chose his lot, maybe he will learn from it, or maybe not" April said.

The job opening that Brock vacated was on the radio, and in the newspaper. In two days a girl who was attending Nursing school was interested in the position. She had grown up on a dairy farm in Wisconsin and was very experienced.

Beth was hired, but now she would be milking evenings and April would milk in the a.m. Beth liked Mrs. Adams, the two of them hit it off! After school Beth cooked a meal for them both and then she did the milking. Sometimes before she left for school she would have the cows tied in for April. Beth was a good worker, dependable and easy to get along with.

That Christmas Beth received a gift of a new car. Beth had been driving something so rickety you could hear her coming. She was so elated she could not believe how kind the Di Angelo's were to her. April explained it was not them it was D Farms that purchased the car for her. She most certainly deserved something good, she had earned this.

Yes, anyone who put forth a good attitude, tried to do their best, was always treated with special kindness of tokens of gratitude. It was all set up this way by April and Arthur from the beginning.

The Meat Stores

THEN THERE WERE THE MEAT STORES. SOMETIMES COWS DIE, LIKE humans. They could have a heart attack, fall and break their leg, or a hip, unable to get up for some unknown reason. Sadly it happens, and the D Farm decided it was far better to use these animals for human consumption then to put in a waste pile. The cows were treated well all the time. They provided milk, time off being dry for their babies to grow. Local farmer's commented that D Farms treated the cows better than most people treat their pet dogs.

When a cow went down, they were humanely butchered. Their meat was made to be "free" for those who were poor, and low cost to others. Each farm had a small brick building in a town with one or two workers. Stocking and dealing with customers.

If a person was poor, (being local would have been known) and if not, they had to provide information by their Doctor or social security office provided for them. It was a small card, credit card size, and a courtesy D Farms provided. D Farms would laminate the cards for them so they would withstand the use. They received up to thirty pound of meat, be it roasts, ribs, cube meat, steaks, chip beef, beef cubes, hot-dogs, chip steak, liver, tail for soup and hamburger every month.

No store kept meat after a month. If there was any meat that old, it was donated to the animal shelters for animal consumption. All of the meat was kept in freezers, not thawed. This meat was stamped organic, no GTMO, no hormones, no antibiotics. The cows ate the organic farm grown corn, soy bean and hay ledge.

They had good alfalfa hay that was made on D farms or pasture grass.

This was quality meat, low fat and delicious. What a blessing to many, many people. Those who were on fixed income, be it middle class or wealthy, there was no discrimination. The meat was for sale to them at a much lower cost than the grocery stores. Purchases were considered a donation, for the loss of the animal.

And it worked, it worked very well, there were never complaints, everyone was happy with this new store, at all sixty five D Farms towns. Many other cities requested that D Farms would come to their area.

April truly believed that dairy farms could end hunger in America. This was exactly what she had tried to explain to Poppo years ago. It was possible if the government did not have so many regulations and restrictions. Their meat was inspected, safe and nutritious for those who used it. Why not donate this meat to the public, offering it at less than half the cost.

April and Author both realized in cities it would be a problem, but it could be managed. April felt if there was a will there was a way. If only, if only it were possible, she needed to think and pray about this. To see if this could be managed this in a safe, sane manner.

Let's Do This Together

THEIR OWN TOWN HAS ITS GROWING PAINS AS WELL. THE DOWN town square needed repairs. The fire department needed a new truck. There was need in the town and April began to go to the town meetings. She was stymied at the salaries those who were elected "earned." They all had full time jobs and were also paid to be on the council?

They lived in the community, they used everything that needed repairs, and felt they should be paid? What ever happened to service? Did they forget service or how to do it? She vowed to herself when she was older this would change.

That February April bought two hundred meat chicks and in three months they were finished for processing. April spoke with the fire department long before this and offered to raise the birds and have a chicken roast.

They would need to have a fire pit made out of cement blocks and a grate on top, roast the birds in half's. When cooked put in a baked potato, a roll, a pat of butter, and a side dish of either macaroni or coleslaw, a carton drink and sell each bag curb side for eight dollars.

Talk about successful, every one supported this. Moms who did not want to cook dinner, people coming out of work on their way home, or people going to work for a good dinner. Often they paid ten dollars for a single meal. They knew the fire department was trying to raise money for a new truck. That effort earned the fire department over Twenty four thousand dollars! Halfway to their goal. April's Dad was in the department as well, and he was elated at the success of this effort.

He spoke to April to see if she was interested in doing it again the late fall, he said that the fire department guys were more than willing to pay for the chicks and feed.

"Then what will I be offering?" she asked. "No, if I am going to help, I am all in. Yes, it is a sacrifice. The cost, the work, the feeding chicks free range them keeping them safe, it is what I want to donate" April said.

Early that fall they did it again, only this time it was five hundred chickens. The chicken dinners were approved to be placed in ads in the newspaper and a small circular flier that came with advertising in the mail. Of course on the radio waves as well, Miranda made sure of that!

They thought outlying areas of Fresno would come, and they did. They were sold out in less than five hours. Now they would have the funds for their truck. With a little innovation, hard work, it was possible to buy most anything without credit. "Work for it" that was April's mantra all throughout her life.

With the success of the fire department, many told April she should run for Mayor next time. April felt that the town needed someone who would be committed, someone who wanted to make a difference for the people in the community. She was going to be fourteen in the following spring and still had commitments of her milking job and the pony rides. She also had set aside three hours a day with Native Son. This would have to wait until she was older. Meanwhile she would help where she could.

The mayor belittled her at every chance he got. April's biggest help was the radio station her Mother now owned.

April never brow beat the Mayor. April spoke on what the Mayor's history was, his record of performance and his attitude towards the people. April said he had a good name but ruined his Fathers reputation of service. "This Mayor was not his Father" she reminded the people. Little by little she would have the people see the Mayor for who he really was.

April promised when she was older would not take a salary, would listen to the concerns of the people and help where she could if they would work with her. Anything was possible if we all work together she said. The results would be known in the next spring elections.

April made an appointment with her family Dr. whom she had known all her life. As Luann put her in the exam room, and closed the door, April sat on the exam table thinking. If only I could control my emotions, not have stress in my life and the Dr. came in, he asked to see her hands. She held them out and he made a clucking sound.

"I have seen them worse than this" he said. "Are you still on the prednisone?" He asked her.

"Yes, I take a full tablet when I feel it beginning to get bad then I decrease it to half. And when it's almost gone, I stop" she said.

"Well you are doing as I told you to. How about coming into my office a week before they race for a steroid shot, that will help keep your hands optimal for the race, it's hard to hold reins with hands like that" he said.

"Must I stay on this, I really don't want to" April said.

"Well, there are creams that might help, we can experiment with that" he told her. "Two percent Hydrocortisone cream would help and a strong hand cream, one that he liked in particular was Norwegian formula.

The Dr. urged her to try the cream when she was going to bed or not using her hands excessively. Like when she was working with cattle or riding, he felt even the dander would bother her.

He wished April good luck as she exited the room ended up at the front again.

"He wants to see you in two weeks" the receptionist said, the appointment was made and April left. She walked to the police department to see her Dad, and get a ride home.

The Preakness Stakes

TWO WEEKS AFTER THE KENTUCKY DERBY WAS THE PREAKNESS Stakes. The next race for Native Son was near. The next race would be held at Pimlico race course in Maryland.

April had ridden Native Son all around town and the men in town would stop their checker game on the store porch to watch her go by. They all liked her. April was really was a good kid. She waved as she went by, as did they. Yes, she conditioned and rested Native Son constantly since the Kentucky Derby two weeks earlier.

Throughout the first race and events after, April lost touch with some of her friends. She missed being with them. One afternoon after conditioning Native Son, April asked her Mother if she would be allowed to have Trevor and Hugh come over. Or maybe she could go and visit with them. Her Mother was glad, April needed some down time. Trevor was away at the movies, but Hugh was home and he was the one who had answered the phone. He said he was making pizzas for dinner and he sure could use some help. Miranda said, "April loves to make Pizza's so I am sure would love to help you." "Ok, I will bring her over."

Hugh and April did make the pizzas and they were delicious, the both moaned that they had eaten too much, laughing at each other.

"Hey, my Grandpa is having a birthday party at the lake, can you come?" Hugh asked.

"Well, I was not invited" April said.

"Oh you know my Grandpa loves you, I sure he would be happy if you came" Hugh said.

"No, I know that my parents would not like it if we were not invited, and I insist we go. That's just how they are" April said.

"Well then I think we should hike over there and ask him Hugh said as he stood up. Besides the walk will do us good" he told her and they got up and went.

They brought along two pieces of pizza wrapped in foil for Grandpa. Hugh put them in a small picnic basket and they headed out. They chatted about everything and anything. Hugh was interested in the D Farms he had heard about and had many questions.

As they walked along April explained the plan, the purpose and results of the D Farms. Hugh was impressed, he never considered such a need or trying to find a solution for college for the poor.

Hugh also questioned her about Brock, what was it she was trying to do with him? Did she have feelings for him?

April felt she had some explaining to do, only because she valued Hugh's friendship, and a good friend worth keeping has the right to know what you are doing.

April told Hugh of Brock's home life, both parents were alcoholics, and his Dad was suspected of drug abuse. It was not a good situation to live in. Brock may have bad influences, and he may want out to develop and change. But that would never happen, unless he had a change of environment.

Work was good it kept your hands and head busy, no time for idleness. That was the reason she tapped Brock, no other.

They soon were at the cabin and Mr. O'Toole was asleep on a chair on the front porch. Hugh winked at April, using his hand to stop and stay still. He quietly put down the basket. He snuck around the back of Grandpa's chair, and rocked it. Grandpa jumped and stood so fast, he looked wild eyed, "It's an earth quake" he hollered. Hugh was laughing so hard, and April began to laugh too. "Oh so ye want to be poking fun at me now are ya?" he said. He knew that Hugh was a practical joker, and he loved that about his Grandson.

And here was that girl he liked so very much, with his Hugh. Now it could not get any sweeter than that.

"Tis good to see you both, what is it that brings you to me home now?" he asked.

"We brought you pizza and have a serious question for you" Hugh told him.

"Put the poison pizza on the table, I'll feed it to the squirrels later today."

Hugh scoffed at him and lifted the basket, "And you did not invite the Di Angelo's to your birthday bash as the lake, so April won't be coming."

"Ah, no, tis not good, tis not good, t'was not me that sent those invites, and if ye did not come lass, I would be sad indeed" he looked at April.

"I know my parents, I could ask or beg and the answer would be no, if they do not get invited, I will not be allowed to go."

"I'll take care of that don't worry your pretty head about it one second more. I would be broken hearted if ye did not come, truly" he told her, and he meant it.

So the next time Mr. O'Toole was in town, he made it his business to stop at the police station and see Mr. Di Angelo. He personally invited Gordon, his wife and daughter to his birthday at the lake. He would not take no for an answer. "We have a lot of time you know, it's in late July" he said.

The Preakenss Stakes

Four days before the Preakness stakes held in (Pimlico) Baltimore Maryland, on May 16th the Di Angelo's left with their van loaded. Native Son was in the lead van with Marty. They decided to take a private train that guaranteed them to be there in two days. Native Son would have his own box stall, and someone would be allowed to stay with him.

Marty said he would stay with him as would Byron, the groom. April said she would. Everyone was against that idea for now, maybe when they were at the track.

The train was awesome, it traveled so fast and the food was delicious, almost like home cooked meals. The beds were small but comfy, and at night sleep came easy with the rocking of the cars.

When they arrived in Maryland there was a box car and a van for their troop.

Native Son was loaded carefully and Byron wanted to ride with him. The Di Anglo's followed in the van.

At the track it was like being home. There were many of the same jockeys there. Native Son folks had two days to settle in and breeze. There were more horses in this race, some they did not know and Marty had homework to do.

The race track at the Preakness Stake was similar to the Kentucky Derby the prize however was for the wood lawn vase. The one mile and 3/16th long track was wet, there had been a soaking rain that night that would make the track slippery for the horses.

Native Son was used to running in most any soil, but not being pushed, bumped or sliding.

It rained and rained some more. Later in the day, Marty came to talk to April about potential problems on the race track and about the riders and horses. His hat was soaked and as he tipped his head forward, a dish full of rain fell off of the front crease.

There was a terrible storm with lightening, and thunder booming. Many of the horses were frightened. Some whinnied, some stomped in their stalls. April stayed with Native Son. She ate her dinner with him as he ate his. April slept in his stall, keeping him calm. The next morning it was doubtful they would run the track. Soon the machinery was out leveling the track, doing what they could to ease off the water.

On the morning of race day, the sun came out and by 1: 00 p.m. all looked good. April knew that the track would not be dry, so she decided to listen to Marty with his opinion.

Marty had walked the entire track and knew where to go in and out throughout the race.

Weighed, dressed and anxiously waiting on her guy Native Son. Bryon brought him to April and Native Son nudged her with is nose, as if to say, "Let's go."

April rubbed his neck. She told him he would have to listen to her reins today. Today he could go and run all he wanted but when she cued with her legs and reins to the left, or right, he had better do it. His great head went up and down, as if he understood. April loved this horse, and win or lose that would never change.

At the starting gate, Native Son was as calm as always. But next to them was a ram charger. That crazy horse would not stand still. He pushed forward and backed against the back stop repeatedly. He pawed and pounded. It was unsettling. April whispered to Native Son to be still and focus. That horse was a bad distraction. They needed to stay away from him. Native Son nickered to her and stood like a soldier at attention.

As they waited in the shoot, April could feel her heart thumping loudly. She re-wound her reins in with her sore hands. April held her breath and prayed. Bam! The gates opened and they were flying out as fast as Native Son could run.

April reined him close to the rail securing the 4th position on the rail. Marty had told her each post where to turn in or out. So at the first quarter she reined him into the middle and then to right. Near the half, she told him to "let it go" and away he went. There was no stopping a freight train like Native Son. When he wanted to move out and run.

It was as if Native Son had another gear, in over drive. Native Son gave all of the effort he had, he just loved to run. As they rounded to the final turn heading home. Native Son was out four lengths. He made a huge statement that day, crossing the finish line on a muddy track in record time.

Again the reporters with cameras came out to the muddy track. Native Sons silks were brown and April was a muddy mess. There was mud on her face, head, and silks. She did not care, she could not have been prouder of Native Son. April leaned forward hugging his neck.

"You did it" April said, to him over and over.

Her Mom came out to the track wading thru mud in her high heels. She had to have the assistance of two men to get to the spot where the horse was. It was a muddy messy day but a wonderful day for the Di Angelo family, Byron, Marty and Native Son.

They would have very little time off, their next race on June 6th, in two weeks. So homeward bound they went. Before they left, April committed to the track ten percent of the earnings and ten percent to tithing.

It was there April met the Proper family, Tia and Mel. They were an older couple. Tia was in a wheel chair and Mel was her constant companion. Tia used to race and show long ago before a car accident that left her no use of her legs. Mel was still involved with horses he had a few of his own and was very active at this track. They instantly hit off a great relationship with April's parents. They made plans to come and visit them after all the races were over. They loved to travel they owned a small motor home that crossed over America.

Homeward bound the Di Angelo family went. Marty insisted that Native Son stay at Arnie's track in Fresno for consistent training. Marty wanted April to ride Native Son every day, on the track and off for conditioning. April was exhausted she asked her parents if she could ask Lauren to stay with the pony rides since she had been doing it for the last two months anyway.

April also wanted out of milking until all the racing was over. Her Dad looked at her with up turned eye brows, as if to say "I told you so" but April pretended she did not see that.

April was more stubborn then either Gordon or his wife. Gordon wondered if her biological mother or father was like that. Later he received a letter in the mail from April's biological Grandfather who wrote. She mirrors my strength, my character in everyway, she brings pride and happiness to my soul with each race. God Speed them and Gordon smiled.

April was not one to back down from anything, in part because of how she was being raised. But a human is much more than a product of their environment. He also knew that genetics played a part in the human body, and he learned much from letters from her Grandfather. April's Great Grand Father had trained horses for the king of Spain.

Gordon knew that horses were in her blood. This was not a mere chance, or a mistake it was her destiny. There would be much good from her in her lifetime and Gordon prayed that April's biological family would live to see much of it.

Getting Ready For The Belmont

BETH GRACIOUSLY AGREED TO DO BOTH MILKING, IN THE MORNING and in the evening. It was more money for her as well. Mrs. Adams also went out to the barn to help Beth. Mrs. Adams got the milk machines ready on the milk cart and she also mixed feed. Mrs. Adams said, "Pushing buttons is not that difficult" It could not have worked out better.

"Just till we get thru June" April thought.

Those next two weeks flew by Native Son was in his prime. He was a three year old stallion that had great ground manners. He was a complete gentleman off the track. On the track he was restless to run.

Their next and last race would be the Belmont Stakes that was one mile and half long track the longest race of the three. It is located in New York. Of course racing your best every two weeks takes toll, and as fit as Native Son was, he was tired, April was felt it when she rode him.

So every night after his work out, he was put in same time. For him to sleep and April was with him every night. It was something she felt she had to do. Marty was in complete agreement with her. They were almost there and needed to do whatever it took to keep Native Son relaxed, rested, and conditioned. After one week of this arrangement and Native Son's eyes looked even brighter, he became more playful wanting to go out and run.

The day they were going to leave, Native Son stepped up on the trailer and his foot slipped off, making a tear along his fetlock, the blood was everywhere.

Marty quickly took off his shirt and made a tourniquet, he had someone call their veterinarian to come quick.

The vet came out and looked at Native Sons fetlock and said, "It is not deep, but I don't know if I would run him hard just yet. When is the race?" He asked.

"In nine days", said Marty.

"He is going to be sore tomorrow, so the travel time is good. Soak his foot if Epson water. Let the area exposed to air, don't wrap it. Keep him on bedding that is clean and dry, try not to get it wet, it needs to be dry. When you get there, let him walk to see how sore it is. If he shows no sign of limping, a light ride at first. Walk the track with him for an hour. If you want to keep conditioning, he will be fine with that."

He was thinking ahead. "By that time it will be five days of healing time. I believe by then you should be able to run him on the track, not full out, enough to keep the foot from getting stiff to keep the blood flowing. Then I believe he will be able to do his best on race day" their vet said. He slapped Marty on his shoulder, "It's always something, isn't it?" and he laughed.

This was a very close call it frightened everyone, except Native Son. He trusted everyone there he had no reason to worry or to be afraid.

They did what the veterinarian asked. They traveled again by rail road. The high speed rail was a blessing. Native son was in his own box car.

Native Son was speeding along to New York, but feeling like he was not moving at all. He loved traveling and he loved his groom Byron who was his constant companion.

Byron loved horses he had been on the tracks since he was a little boy, following in his Dad's footsteps. Two years earlier, his Daddy had a bad accident at the track and was fired. Since then money was tight in their home with four other children to feed.

Bryon's Dad was able to secure a job, but he struggled. The minute Manny and April met Byron they knew right away he would be good for Native Son. Byron had a jovial attitude. He was always happy, smiling and bringing a good feeling every day of the week. For the circumstances with his family, he did not let that get in his way. He chose to be happy no matter what. For that reason, the Di Angelo's and Marty tapped Byron out to be with them. Arthur sent out weekly checks to Byron's family. Every two weeks Byron was given an envelope with cash, he was delighted.

When they arrived in New York, Native Son showed no slightness in his walking. But they continued to follow the veterinarian's advice. Again April stayed with Native Son. Two days before the race April was walking that track with Native Son for hours. They were being sought after and then laughed at by other horse owners. The reporters wanted her to run him and she ignored them

They did not know, and they had no reason to know, if they had they would use it against them. The thing was April did not understand why people chose to be mean to get ahead.

You can be kind and win and get ahead too. Why didn't they want to be helpful? They wanted only what they wanted, instead of being kind and getting along? It was that way with man. April wanted no part of it, so she chose to keep to herself and her group.

Two days before the race, April brought Native Son out to breeze him. He showed no slightness in his foot. Because April was holding him back. He began to paw with that injured foot to go.

April did not want to let him full out, they cantered around that track for five laps. She knew she had to hold him in and it was a bit of a tussle. April had to pull his reins in and talk to him. He would shake his head as if in disagreement and pull his head forward to be let out. But she could not let him, not yet. That breeze was not much fun at all, not for either of them. The reporters were at the rail heckling them. That irritated April most of all.

The day before the race, was the day she opened him up. The rest did him well. He was riveting with energy and she could feel him the tense ripples under her. On Marty's advice she opened him up, it was great. He steamed past spectators and reporters like the wind, he was ready.

After the breeze, April wanted to wash Native Son herself. Usually Bryon washed him at the tracks. At home he was washed and sang to by April almost every night. April grabbed a bucket and soap, some sponges, turned on the radio and began to hose him down. She washed him and Native Son loved his baths. He would stretch his back when you were scrubbing it. He did not mind his face washed, sometimes he would open his mouth for you to hose out his mouth with water.

He was such a clown sometimes. Just then a song came on the radio that April liked very much. When it came on, she began to animate dancing to Native Son as if he were the object of her affection. April would point at him and sing, "I know you want to leave me, but I refuse to let you go." She danced around him as she washed him, spinning and dancing. Soon some of the grooms at the track were watching her.

Then one grabbed a video camera and began recording. That recording became a source of laughter to April for years to come. It also marked a time of innocence. April did not have a boyfriend, and she did not go out on dates. Native Son owned her heart.

As she sang, "I refuse to let you go, if I have to beg sweet daring" Yes, the horse was quite animated as well. He would lift his head as if he were responding. His tongue would roll out with his mouth opened. It was quite funny indeed. April washed and danced and spun, sprayed the hose water on him. They both were wet with soap and water and had a wonderful time. Just as if they were home in their own yard. And that simple task, relaxed Native Son. He was not stressed at all. It was as if all were well. They were not at home, but it seemed like home. He was ready.

The Belmont Race

ON BELMONT STAKE'S RACE DAY, APRIL WEIGHED IN GOT DRESSED and headed out for her guy, and there was Tia and Mel. They were rooting for her and wanted her to know. "You know if he wins this race, he will be a Triple Crown Winner" Tia said excitedly.

"Yes, I know but I push that thought away, it's a race, just like any other race, one by one" April replied.

"Good for you" Mel said patting her shoulder, "That's the way to look at it, one race at a time."

April thanked them and excused herself, it was time to go, she kissed Tia on her forehead and left. Tia was very touched no one paid her much attention since her accident. There was a time she could command a crowd, but anymore, she was almost invisible.

For some reason this small girl saw her, she did not know why but it was nice to be recognized, seen and treated kindly. Tia suspected it was April's up-bringing. he liked the Di Angelo's immensely. They were calm sensible parents she felt that had a lot to do with April's actions.

Marty lifted April to the saddle and reminded her for the last time to watch for two riders and their horses. He looked directly into her eyes as he said it. Her Dad made sure her feet were in the stirrups correctly. Byron turned Native Son and they began their ride towards the track.

They did not have an escort of another horse and rider, April preferred not to. It was always her and Native Son. She did not need anyone else.

As they rode they heard cheers, and hopeful chants for them to become the next Triple Crown Winner. April did the best she could to push that thought far out of her mind. This was just another race, a race he could win if they worked together.

April kept her eyes on the two horses Marty told her about. April knew the track was solid, firm but not dusty. She knew that there were no soft spots and that if she could keep clear from the two horses Manny told her about, they would be alright. They'd have a good chance.

You see when you are a winner you are the one they are after. You are the one to beat!

The ride to the shoots went quick. Native Son entered his entry like a gentleman. The white horse Marty warned her about was next to them on their left. He was a white maniac. He kept trying to put his head over to Native Son and bite him. His rider did not restrain him or try to stop him. On the third time when that horse did that, April punched the horse in the side jaw area. His jockey said something to her in another language. April said, "You make him behave, or I will."

The other side was dingdong, all the way down on the far end of the entry gates, nowhere near them. That is until the bell sounded. Native Son never hesitated when those shoots opened. He bolted out and there beside them on their left were the white maniac and then on the right was the bay dingdong coming straight at them. April and Native Son were going to be sandwiched in between them. April leaned forward urging him to move faster, which she never did before. April moved him to the right, to the left, to the middle and then to the right again.

Native Son loved to run on the outside, but that was just where they expected him to be, and April could not afford that. So she let him run on the inside, until the last quarter of the track was past them. Then she reined him right to the outside and told him to "Let it go" and he did.

Native Son gathered speed passing the horses to his left and right, and in eight strides he broke free and no one was near him. He kept increasing his speed and stride until he was three lengths in front and as April looked over her left shoulder she saw the white maniac coming for her. The horse was being whipped repeatedly, and beside him was the dingdong bay, he seemed to running out of sheer terror, wild eyed. Neither of these two horses ran because they liked it.

April turned her head back and hollered to her horse "Come on boy" "Move!" Native Son kicked in the highest gear he had, his stride lengthened and he moved twice as fast.

Native Son finished three and a half lengths ahead of the pack. It was a hard earned race, for him. As they slowed their run around the track April leaned to the side to check his fetlock. It seemed ok she could not see red or blood.

April and Native Son headed to the winners circle and there were her parents, Manny and Bryon grinning from ear to ear. Her Mom however, had tissues wadded in her hands and they were stuffed in her jacket pockets, which made April smile.

The owner of the track came out, the announcer and everyone, like an entourage, it was a big deal!

As always small speeches, congratulations all around, it was so exciting and she wanted to live this moment forever, and then it was all done! Native Son was featured in all the sports magazines, in newspapers, it was amazing.

After the race it was a blur to April. It all happened so fast, and it was stressful. It left not much to think about. She was tired, no exhausted. They all were. All except Native Son, his conditioning and rest helped him immensely.

Hold On A Minute

However, for April it was a story altogether different. The press showed pictures of April's behind bent over her saddle to show her entire back side. They took pictures of her with her hair down riding Native Son, featuring her as "hot". April got upset. She had no idea where they got this idea! She never came across as immoral or risque'.

What right did these publishers have to show her in that way? April was determined to call every one of them and make them apologize. She wanted them to put in a different set of pictures that show the truth. April followed through and did just that. She made them hear her. April would travel to their offices and of course they wanted an interview with the Triple Crown winning rider and owner of Naïve Son.

It was on her terms, a retraction, and apology. They had to come to their farm and take pictures of her and who she really was. April was a home town, home grown girl on the farm, and on the track.

It was good she did, she never wanted to project a bad image of herself. It did matter what people thought, but the person it mattered most to, was the girl in the mirror.

April loved her family and wanted them to be thought of and remembered as being good, because they were really good.

April would never have been satisfied to just let it go it concerned her enough to make it right. They all got it! They understood, and were kind enough, wise enough to do a retraction, re shoot another story, the real one.

Reporters Day!

April's Parents called it Reporters Day! They hosted a pit barbeque with steaks or hamburgers, all sorts of side dishes. Corn on the cob, salads, all outside around the fire pit, Gordon had built. Many came! They all were treated like family. Candid photos were taken that were endearing. April offered to take some of them horseback riding. They were brave souls taking her up on her offer. April never was tempted to run the horses they walked the trail, cameras taking pictures all the while.

The magazines after that day were much better pictures, capturing the beauty of the land, the down to earth, humble person April truly was. It showed her connection with Native Son and the other animals on their farm. They all left as friends, and it remained that way.

Some would stop years later asking if the Di Angelo's if they remembered them, which they did. Then they would tell them of their new job or assignment, where they would be traveling or if they stayed in work of photographic shoots, or into family life.

As April ventured into other lines of business, she called on some of the photography people to do photo shoots for her. There is never any sense to burning bridges sometimes feelings erupt to the surface. Hopefully adults can make decisions that are fair.

It is unfortunate when people do not put themselves in the other person's shoes, if they would, many arguments and disagreements would be resolved. There would be less grudges, or resentments.

It was now late June, and with the races behind her she breathed, truly breathed, taking in everything at home and around her.

Bagpipes

April always loved it here. From the first time she sat in the police cruiser, timid and afraid, she saw Gordon's farm from a window. But April did not appreciate it all as she did right now. Poor little Ruby almost went dizzy circling around April's feet for attention, that was a statement of how long April had been away.

April knew that the Mayor race would not begin until next fall. The birthday party at the lake for Mr. O'Toole was in the last part of July and she had an idea to discuss with her Mother.

"Bag pipes?" Miranda questioned her. "Yes, I want to learn to play, so I can play them for Mr. O'Toole at his birthday" April answered her.

And Miranda did in deed find an old soul who was twenty four years old he was in an Irish band in college. He willingly gave April lessons, every single day! Miranda brought him a good meal everyday along with some money for his time and talents. The money was useful, but the meals were priceless, he truly appreciated them. Unfortunately he had to leave town in two weeks, so Miranda went hunting. She was successful finding a man who played checkers at the local store. His name was Mr. Balley.

The end of July rolled around, the hay was made, the straw baled, and put in all the barn lofts, April imagined this was happening all across America, at the D Farms.

April went one afternoon to see Arthur, their faithful accountant. There he was in the office downtown, bent over his desk, with paperwork neatly stacked in separate bins.

She brought him a frozen soda it had been an extremely hot day. "So, how are you?" April asked him

"I am good, and have good news for you" he said excitedly taking the frozen soda, taking a sip saying, "Awe, that's good, thanks so much."

"Well, you are now up to 210 farms across America each one represents a dairy of 200 or more cows that are milked twice a day. He winked at her because she knew that. The milk prices are good, and there have been no accidents or problems all year nowhere!" He said. April was relieved, it was almost a miracle. But then, all of the workers did attend church. That was a requirement and that she thought was the main reason there was harmony. They had a good half hours talk, everything was good.

April asked where he was taking his family on vacation that year. "Oh we are not going anywhere, my wife's condition is not such that she can travel and I am gone away so often with the farm purchases, I prefer to stay home" he said.

"Nope" April said, "You are all going somewhere, your wife needs to get out and feel the sun and air. I know she will enjoy it, besides I need you fresh from time to time. You are getting circles under your eyes" she laughed at him. "Yes, I suppose I am" he said, "but",… "Absolutely no but's" April said, "I will take care of everything" which left him speechless.

April left and went to Author's home. The tending Nurse was there with his wife. It was the Nurse who answered the door. "Come in" she said, as April spoke with Diane.

Diane expressed a desire to see the ocean to feel the breeze of the wind on her face and sand on her feet. April asked her Nurse if she would like to go on vacation too, "Oh my, why not?" She answered. April told her consider it done. So with the help of her Mother, they booked a two week vacation. It was at one of the nicest posh hotels in California near a beach. Everything was provided as was the funds for meals, entertainment and travel.

To the Di Angelo's Arthur and his family were indispensable they could not manage without them. April was excited to have helped plan a nice vacation for such nice people. She just knew all of them would get some much needed rest and relaxation, and some fun time too, exactly what they all needed.

As for April she was back to milking the cows at 4 a.m. and then pony rides at 10 a.m. then feeding all of the calves. Native son was still at Arnie's getting the royal treatment. They were offering breeding from the Triple Crown winner. Gordon thought that they should buy a mare for breeding. Use him as stud and rebreed Native Sons mother with a notable sire to see what they might get.

April focused elsewhere the bag pipe playing was so cool. She wanted to learn two songs, Loch Lomond and the Irish Lullaby on this instrument. Bagpipes were a difficult instrument to learn and took a lot of breath. April practiced every chance she got with Mr. Balley. He was patient and persistent teaching her the two songs she most wanted to play. April told Hugh the songs she had in mind to play and he told her that the one was his Grandmothers favorite song, "The Irish Lullaby."

Her playing just about drove the Di Angelo's crazy all that wheezing, and humming. April's parents were patient. Miranda bought ear plugs they wore evenings as April practiced. They give up watching television and read a lot. It was just a matter of time and April would be done with this, so they hoped.

The end July came, the picnic bash at the lake was sure to be the event of the year. The lake was filled with boats. There was one boat that if you chose to perform for the Birthday boy, you would enter on the gangplank. Then walk onto the deck of the boat. There were spot lights from the masts that would shine on you and if you did well, a green light would shine from the O'Toole's deck. That would mean you did well and you were invited to his Birthday bash.

It was a tough competition, well not to each other but to be approved by the O'Toole's. Some kids told jokes, and they were funny, but no green light. Some played guitar and banjo together, which April thought they did very well, but no green light. April began to be jittery and Hugh was with her, "Don't get nervous, you will do well I know you will, and besides you are invited anyway" Hugh said.

"I know, but I want him to be pleased" she said.

"Oh he will, especially if he knows it's you" Hugh said. "I don't want him to know it's me" April said, "I want to win a spot in his heart."

Hugh thought to himself, you already have girl, you already have.

It was April's turn she was wearing a long white cotton dress, with cap shoulders.

She had three quarter sleeves and a white shawl that the tassels blew in the night wind. She wore a head cover so no one on the hill would know who she was.

As April stepped onto the deck of that yacht the deck was a little slippery and one of the men noticed and got a towel wiping it dry for her. April stepped up and shouldered her bagpipes and began to pipe "The Irish Lullaby". It came out beautiful, strong and pure. It was as if the music floated over the water, into the evening air up to the sparkling lights. Everyone was quiet there was no talking, only that pure bag pipe music floating around them, evoking tears in many.

April stopped when it was over, she began to pipe and then sang, "Too Ra Loo Ra Loo Ra Too Ra Loo Ra Li, Hush Now Don't You Cry. As she sang, Mr. O'Toole was captured. He said loudly to everyone, to hush! There was not a sound on his deck or household. Everyone crept closer to see who this was singing this Irish Lullaby with such emotion, such depth of her soul.

They could not see her face. They only heard the clear meaning of the words in her song as she played her bagpipes. "You take the high road and I'll take the low road and I'll be in Scotland afore ye, for me and my true love will never meet again, on the Bonnie, Bonnie banks of Loch Lomond." Mr. O'Toole was crying like a baby, he wiped his face and the tears kept coming. That was his sweetheart and his favorite song. When they were first married they would sing it together on walks, or on rides in his car. She was gone near thirty years now, and the emotions of that young voice pierced his heart.

He felt like he was twenty four again, full of life and love for his sweetheart.

As the young singer ended she stood there with her head bowed. It was silent no one said anything, and no green light. Soon the boats in the lake began to honk their horns, and people began to shout, "More, sing some more." April did not know what to do she was not prepared to sing more. April stood there and then suddenly in the haze of the lake the green light came on. The crowd erupted in clapping and cheers, many more horns on the boats began to honk.

Hugh was the official on and off with people appointee, he assisted April off and said, "You did it, I just knew you would, and he did not know who you were." April smiled at him and hugged him, "You were right Hugh, I am so glad you were here with me tonight, can you come with me up the hill up to your Grandfathers?" she asked him.

Hugh looked around and there was another man who was willing to do his job for him, no words were exchanged. Hugh just nodded his head.

They got on dinghy that was owned by a cousin of his and that man took them to the other side of the lake so they could climb the stairs to the O'Toole's home. April and Hugh were both familiar with these stairs they had climbed them so many times.

Coming along behind them were April's parents, she could hear her Mother complain she could not see. April began to laugh as did Hugh.

They did not mean to make fun of Miranda she had a very difficult time seeing in the dark and then to the water's edge. The brush and weeds reached to the long flight of stairs.

Hugh and April waited for them at the landing. Miranda hugged her daughter. April held a finger to her lips, and they continued on. April heard her Dad tell Mr. O'Toole they were glad to be there. He had to work and was a little late but so glad to have come. It was such a beautiful lake with all the boats on it tonight and the people were all friendly and kind. As April and Hugh came up the deck Hugh was in front of her, blocking her from his Grandfather's sight.

"Who do you have there now Hugh my boy, is that the singer now?"

"It is Grandpa" Hugh said and he stepped aside. April put her head piece down to reveal it was her. Mr. O'Toole clapped and put his hands along both sides of his face and then he motioned for April to come to him and he enveloped her in a hug.

As he hugged her he whispered to her, "Ye have captured me heart darlin' I was moved to tears and so grateful for the beautiful memory, truly, and I thank you."

April looked at him and said, "I wanted to surprise you and give you a good Birthday gift. I wanted to win your approval."

"Oh darlin' you did that and he laughed and hugged her again.

Mrs. Marshall came to April and hugged her, "You have a beautiful voice April, we video tape the people on the yacht and we will make a copy for you to have."

"How ever did you learn the bagpipes, it is something my Dad always wanted me to learn and I could not get the hang of it" she said.

"Oh I like the bagpipes they are a little awkward, but I love the sound they make" April replied.

Mrs. Marshall patted April's shoulder, "You're a better person than I am, I just didn't like them." April took Mrs. Marshall's hand and squeezed it. The woman looked at her saying "You fit right into this clan" she looked at her father, Mr. O'Toole who was nodding in agreement.

Soon the Di Angelo's had a plate of food and they sat on seats at the back side of the lawn. April sat there looking at the people she knew many of them, but many she had never seen before.

Some came up to her and asked about the races she had won. Some were curious who she was and how she knew the O'Toole's. She just told them she won the green light. She did not need to tell about her life.

And then there was Hugh. He was so tall and handsome. So friendly and nice, full of jokes, and April realized she more than "liked" Hugh. April began to have feeling for him. She did not want to, she shook her head, but it was there. She felt her heart tweak and she could not stop it. Hugh came to sit with her and she flushed red, "Are you alright, do you want a cool drink of soda or water?" he asked her.

"No, I am alright, and it's nice of you to offer, you're such a good friend to me" April said, wondering what he would say to her.

"Well I like you April you're a lot like me, you don't chase after people.

Some girls follow me around like I am a puppy they are trying to catch and I don't like it at all. If I want to talk to a girl I will. If I don't want to, I walk away and that's that. You understand me, don't you April?" He asked her.

"Oh I think I do and it's your right, you know, to talk to whomever you want to. Maybe it would be best to say, excuse me I am busy or excuse me I have to go. Maybe then they would let you alone" she answered him.

He sat there beside her and took her hand in his, she felt her heart jump and her pulse race, "Oh man I hope he does not notice" she thought. He did not seem to, Hugh was pointing out people he knew that she did not. As she watched him, she took in his face, the outline of his strong jaw. She would smile from time to time. She felt like she was powerless, so she quickly stood up and said, "Gosh I wish I could go swimming!"

Hugh looked at her surprised, "Really, ok then let's go" and away they went for their bathing suits. April was relieved to be up and moving. Hugh could swim like he was born in the water, so strong, and agile. April knew she was in trouble. She and her Mother had this talk long ago, and she laughed at her Mother. "No boy is going to look at me" she said. And in part, she was right it was HER looking at Hugh. "I just can't stop it" she said out loud.

"Stop what?" Hugh asked. Thinking quickly she said, "I had a Charlie horse in my leg." Hugh said, "I saw you running the three point lane, I do it too when I can, that builds muscle you know. So that's probably why.

Let's swim for a while maybe that will help, or we can sit on the piling dock too." All April wanted to do was disappear she did not want Hugh to know how she felt, this was so lame! Agh! April was screaming inside.

They swam, they rested, and Hugh picked up her leg on the piling dock asking, "Does it hurt here?"

"Oh no, it actually feels much better" April said. She felt her heart race and her face flush, and she slipped in to the water underneath to hide her reactions. She hoped Hugh had not noticed. Hugh watcher her and he thought she was just amazing. April was the nicest girl he knew. She liked to run, loved community service, got along with his parents and his Grandpa. Yes, she was the girl for him, but he did not want anyone to know. Not even her, not for a while anyway.

Olympics Again?

AN OLDER WOMAN CAME TO TALK TO HER PARENTS. SHE WAS involved with the ski and skating winter Olympic committee and was wondering if April would be interested in joining them. Gordon's head began to reel. April had just come home, and now there was another adventure lying at their feet. "Yes, we would be interested in speaking to you, but if you please" Gordon asked her. "Could we do it at another time, perhaps you could stop by our home some evening or on a weekend. We get away so little it is nice to enjoy the evening together as a family". The woman was in complete agreement and she took their address Gordon wrote down and went to the Marshall senior.

April had no clue someone wanted to change her life again, she was quite content to be back home. Her schedule was full, getting up at sat 4 a.m. to feed, the calves and ponies, that took two hours. She usually could catch a ride with her Dad. Often she had breakfast with him. Then she grabbed her book bag and clothes bag, kissing her Mother good day repeating, "God does not make junk" and leaving.

Her Dad would drop her off at Arties and she would work and train with Native Son for an hour and a half or two hours sometimes. School started at 8:10 am, Arnie would drive her to the school area on the road and April would get out, cross the road to get to the school. From 8:10 a.m. to 2:00 p.m.

April had permission to leave early to feed animals and went to Mrs. Adams to do the PM milking. From 3:00 to 5:30 she was there in the milking barn.

When finished, she mixed feed. Then she let the cows out, making sure the milk machines were set to wash. Last was scraping the path way of the barn, for the next morning so it would be dry. Often she was done before her Dad came by to get her. But sometimes she was pulling a calf or treating a dry cow, or the varying needs of the animals.

When April and Dad got home, they fed the ponies right away. That was easy. They pitched dry hay to them on the dry lot and making sure their water source was clean, no hay, dirt or bugs in it.

Yes, April liked her life as it was. She had reading to do for next year, and she felt such appreciation for everything. April did keep practicing the pipes, guitar and violin evenings outside often with her Dad.

Every Wednesday night she had youth night at the church since. April loved the Young Women's Program. It had so many areas to study and grow in. April also liked all of the girls who were there. They were all so different, and many had problems like many girls do, but they handled them with prayers, scripture and patience.

It was an evening of games, activities and sometimes scripture study for kids ages 12 to 18. She liked many of the kids there. Not all of them went to church with her. Some were from school wanting something to do and that was so cool for them to come. Even Trevor and Hugh came.

The leaders often planned events for them to go to. Some cost money and some cost nothing. They played volleyball, kickball, picked garbage off the roads.

They did service projects for elderly people. Cleaning

rain gutters from leaves, raking lawns, it was always a night of "working together." It was fun for her. She got to know many of the town people this way.

Often April would end up working beside Hugh on service projects because others gave up, or were sweaty or tired. Hugh and April were workers and liked to get things done.

On fun activities they would challenge each other, laugh at each other and the older girls thought they were so childish. Hugh would laugh at them saying, "We are having a great time, what about you?" The three of them were often seen together and they all got along like close family.

April felt she had to be careful she did not want to do anything that would change the relationship between her and Hugh. She valued his friendship immensely and never wanted to lose him as a friend. Trevor was less mature than April was and he often teased his older brother that he was in love with April. Hugh would run his hand from the top of Trevor's head to the bottom of his face, saying, "Get out of here" and laugh at him. But Trevor was not crazy, he saw what he saw and he believed that his brother liked April a lot, a lot more then he let on.

In the previous fall when April stayed after school to learn about the gymnastic program the school had. April thought she was joining kind of late, because some of the gymnast kids were in since age three. April learned many tumbling moves, how to vault, the balance beam which she liked very much. The uneven parallel bars, and floor exercise, which were dance routines with gymnastic moves.

The gym instructor was a woman and she did help all of the kids, but she had her favorites. Those whom she felt would win.

That was fine with April. Some of the girls were frustrated but when they worked together they could accomplish their goals

April learned that Vicky was in this group, the Mayor's daughter. Vicky was a very pretty girl and a spoiled girl. She was not very athletic but she had the nicest Jan sport clothing you ever saw with the brightest colors. April set her mind to get along, not suck up to her, but get along.

So from that day all throughout the year April worked out in the gym and at home, practicing. She loved all of the apparatus, she had fallen many, many times and would laugh at herself, "Room for improvement."

The next fall would be the tri meet of several schools, and April's school coach wanted her to enter in all around. Vicky and several other girls were as well. April did not want personal attacks from her teammates, mainly Vicky. Ultimately she was going to do her best to try to win. April hoped they would all be supportive of one another, for the team to try to win as well. Fall all was months away, for now she had time to hone her skills, and learn.

Her Dad picked her up one evening and told her about the woman who approached him at the O' Toole birthday bash. April was curious and wanted to know what it was about so Dad said he could call her that evening and he did. What this entailed was the Winter Games was in need of an alternate that could be used for Ski racing, or maybe the jump. Only if someone got hurt or could not compete would they need her. There were other options, but for sure they were looking for someone who could ski well, and not afraid of heights. She told Gordon April could stay with a family in Poland who had milking goats who did need help. The father had injured his arm and was not able to milk his goats. His two sons were speed skaters and he did not want to impede their chances for a medal.

April thought this was nuts, why couldn't they help out and then ski or skate? The woman said she would stop by their home within the month. Well that is what she would do, but for now there were things to do here at home. The Gymnastic meet was in the fall. Then after that she could go "if" her parents and April were both in agreement.

After several months the meet in Gymnastics was here. All throughout the training, Vicky was nasty, making nasty comments, just far enough away so April could not hear it all. But always close enough for April to hear her name. On one such occasion April walked up to Vicky, tapped her on the shoulder and said, "If you have something you'd like to say to me, or about me, how about saying it to my face?"

Vicky just smiled a catty smile and said, "Oh, it's nothing for you to worry about, you wouldn't understand it anyway" and laughed.

April felt sorry for Vicky she had to always put people down to feel she was superior.

Bullies

THE WORLD'S VIEW OF BULLYING IS TO AVOID THEM, GO AND TELL your parents or someone in authority. Those are good ideas. But you must, must stand up for yourself. Find the inner strength, to take care of yourself. The best way you know how, by telling, seeking help, staying away.

For April, she was one with the nature to directly confront bullies. She had been picked on at home, but by much bigger people and was helpless. But with Vicky, this was a no brainer. April had to stand up to Vicky. Restate what Vicky said. April felt Vicky did not realize half of what she was saying. April would tell her honestly her feelings and make it clear to stop or there would be firm consequences.

Bullies talk smack, put people down, or take it out physically, emotionally, verbally or on line, which all are very, very wrong. All too often kids are not mature enough or able to deal with what lies are said, afraid others will believe it. No one has a right to touch you.

Bullies themselves are not happy people, they are often picked on, at home, in a job, and they act out against others. All learned from example from their bullies. And that causes frustration. Bullying is often shown on television in violent movies, games. Never ever will bullying end. Adults are bullies. The government can bully, animals bully one another.

Bullying is a part of a violent nature that if they are not taught better, not to bully, it will never end.

Not so long as there are people, not robots, that is the nature of man. His selfishness it is difficult to change, and often they just plain don't want to.

The Gymnastic Tri-Meet

THE TRI MEET DATE CAME. THERE WERE MANY SCHOOLS participating. Some of the girls were in one event, and some were in more. Each school did have several girls in the "all around", competition.

There were always events going on, all at the same time. The spring board and horse had action as did the floor routines. April loved the balance beam and she was good on it. April did tumbling to aerial stunts. She kept a positive attitude even when she made a mistake. All of the girls encouraged one another, especially the younger girls. Each one had different strengths. No one had the same skills.

As the day progressed, April knew some of the girls from other schools were much better on several of the apparatus than she was. That's life! You can prepare all you can and someone may come along and beat you. But April knew the balance beam she was solid. She stuck like glue while she did her routine. The pommel she flew over and was able to stick her landing. The uneven parallel bars were like flying, she could change up and cross over, let go and reclaim that bar.

April felt her routine was strong she would have to wait and see.

The floor exercise was the most dramatic of all, full of expression and feeling. April imagined some of the other girls might think they were good at this too. It was all in the performance and in the Judge's hands. April performed well, as good as she felt she could, and at the end of that very long, long day, she ended up in the finals. She tied for all round champion with another girl from another school.

April was thrilled, there was only one trophy. April gladly let the other girl have the big trophy to take home. The tri meet was in her town and she knew she would eventually get another one. Miranda would have the task of wondering where to put the big trophy anyway.

April was giddy, she laughed to herself. Mr. O'Toole was right, running was therapy but also put her in great condition. Often she ran with Hugh. She also liked running with the Captain. He was retired from the military but ran every day, and he was a great running partner. Even though he was near 70 years old. He said running kept him young.

On the way home April thought she'd go to the farm where Native Son was. She knew her Mom was at a Relief Society meeting and Dad was helping someone with their car. April began to walk that stretch of highway then she noticed headlights coming her way. She walked close to the guide rail and she did have reflective clothing on.

The car kept coming but it was not in the correct lane. The car was more in the center of the road. As April watched a car passed her on her right side heading toward the other car coming from the other direction. She hoped the first car would correct and get over.

April kept walking, looking down every now and then, it was dark now. She clicked on the light she kept on her hat brim it had a bright beam.

The Horrible Accident

As April walked along, in a matter of minutes she heard a very loud crash. A screeching like metal being dragged, lights beaming into the sky and then nothing. Absolute dead silence.

April began to run, she ran and ran to the spot where she thought the cars were and there was nothing on the road. Some metal, some glass, but the cars were gone. April looked down to the right side of the road, the guide rail had been torn away, and as she peered down the side she saw the wreckage of two cars, steam and smoke.

April pulled off her jacket, keeping her hat and light, and began to climb down the side of the road to where the cars were. She held onto rocks, cement, and small trees, until she reached the bottom. The one car had an elderly woman inside who was coherent and talking. She kept asking about Alice and Ernest, who were her passengers with her. Alice was alright, she was breathing but not awake. Ernest did not make it. He had a huge gash in the side of his head, blood was everywhere. To be sure, April checked for his pulse, there was none.

April asked Grace if she could get out of the car. Grace said she felt alright, so April opened the car door and helped Grace move her legs to the outside of the car. She helped Grace, and told her to hold onto her putting the woman's hands around April's neck.

Ever so slowly, carefully, step by step. April climbed to the top of the road with Grace holding onto her. She set Grace at the bridge five feet from where the accident had happened. April climbed back down and helped Alice the same way.

Back down again to the second car. To her shock it was Vicky sitting in the driver's seat. She was not moving, not breathing. She had no blood on her Vicky looked like she was asleep when April saw the clutch ball had impaled Vicky's side. Her side was open and blood and her intestines were on the clutch and floor.

There were four other girls with Vicky, who were all crying, hurt, confused and dazed. They said Vicky argued with them "She was going to drive" Vicky was not old enough to have a license, not even a permit, but she bullied and got her way.

They had been singing to a song on the radio when Vicky lost control. They did not have time to stop her or turn the wheel. One by one, April had each girl, climb with her, or carry them to the top to the older women.

When the last girl was up, April was able to flag down the first car that came near them, asking them for help. It happened to be a man she knew from town. He was the owner of the sports bar, and Chuck quickly got on his CB radio for help. There was a pickup truck that came along behind Chuck and the two of them put the older women and girls on the back of the pickup truck and headed to the hospital in town.

April rode along on the back with them, covering them with blankets Chuck had in his car and her jacket.

The girls were all crying and afraid, only one of them had had a driver's license and she said Vicky kept after her to let her drive.

"I didn't want to do it, I tried to tell her no but Vicky would not listen to me, she took my keys and, and well here we are now, without her." She began to cry again. It was a sad ride, no one really said anything. The girls kept crying. April scooted over to them and told them, "You must say Vicky pulled at the wheel that is all I am asking of you.

She is gone let's try to spare her family."

The two women clung to each other and April reached over and touched them, asking if they were alright. They both shook their heads yes. They said they were on their way home from dinner, three friends out for a nice night. Now Ernest was gone. April felt so bad for them.

They arrived at the hospital and April jumped off the back of the truck. "You all stay here I am going to get help." She went inside asking for gurneys and wheel chairs. April also asked someone to call her Dad and have him come out to the hospital as soon as he could. April then went out and helped each one as she could. Gordon Di Angelo arrived as the last girl was put in a wheel chair and taken into the hospital. When April saw him, she ran to him hugging him, "Oh Dad, I am so glad you came" and she told him what had happened. April did not say one word about who was driving that other car he would find that out for himself.

Gordon asked his daughter to take him to where the accident had happened, as they got into the squad car two other deputies came in their cars to assist.

As they drove along, April told her Dad to slow down, and there it was the big black spot on the road and missing guide rail. Gordon got out and shone his flashlight to the two cars down below. "How did they get out of down there?" he asked.

"I carried them out, on my back" April said. Gordon looked at his daughter and was speechless. He motioned for the deputies to go with him down to see the scene. April did not go down, she waited up top, waiting and crying, "What would they say to Vicky's father?"

Gordon hollered up to her, "Did you see who was driving the second car April?" "No, no I did not" she replied.

Because April did not let Vicky in the driver's seat, she pulled her over onto the passenger side, turning her body as if she had been turning around to talk to someone in the back seat. Allowing the clutch to reach her and impale her causing all the damage. April did not want the Mayor to suffer a blow like this. It was bad enough his daughter was gone, he did not deserve a scandal or to endure the talk. That reason is why she moved Vicky's body. Not to cover up evidence, nothing would bring Vicky back. In this way no charges would come against Vicky or her family. She pulled the wheel, it was all an accident.

Deep inside Gordon Di Angelo knew that something was not right. It did not look suspicious but deep inside he felt something was wrong. They all came up together. A call was made to the coroner to come out. April stood by her Dad's squad car waiting. Gordon walked to his daughter, putting his arms around her, "Are you alright?" he asked her.

"I am" she said, with tears.

"Ok, I am going to take you home and then we will need to get this cleaned up" he said.

He spoke to his deputies, telling them procedure and he would be back in a little bit. On that ride, her Dad asked her, "Did you move Vicky's body?"

"Yes, I did. I am not going to lie. I do not want any more pain for her family. It's over, Vicky is no more. Nothing will bring her back. No amount of money. Their family will suffer because of her death not because of what I did."

And nothing ever did come of it. At graduation Vicky received honors posthumously, and her parents were very proud. And that trophy April won in that tri-meet? April gave to the school in Vicky's honor.

The Skating Party

THE WOMAN DID STOP AT THE DI ANGELO'S HOME. HER NAME WAS Gail she was an older woman in her late 60's with long dark hair she kept in a ponytail, under a cap. Gail felt that April was a natural athlete from what she saw of her riding, running the cross country miles on their farm property trails and in gymnastics. Gail wanted April to come and train with them for cross country skiing. April could live with a family who were not as affluent as the Di Angelo's and train with their sons, who were Olympic Speed skaters.

The Di Angelo's agonized over this talk with April, but if she were to do it, she should do it soon. She would be older in the spring, at the time when the Olympics would be happening. Then when they were over she would have time to work with Native Son again.

April would have to leave, she'd have months to train and then compete. It was rushing things, but April always liked it like that, she always jumped both feet in never hesitating.

It was now November the ponds were frozen and all of the Young Women wanted to go ice skating.

That week Miranda needed help cleaning leaves from the gutters, the birds had been making nests in them and she asked in church if someone would help her remove them. Both her husband and daughter were not home much to help. Mrs. Marshall volunteered Hugh, she said he would be happy to come over and help. It was on a windy Saturday when Hugh pulled up in his dad's pick-up truck. He got out and knocked on the Di Angelo's door.

Miranda greeted him fondly, "Hello Hugh, how are you?" she asked him.

"Oh, I am fine" he was looking around, "Is April at home? He asked.

"No it is Saturday and they left out for a two hour ride today, there were about thirty riders, so I don't expect them back before 2:00 today. "Oh, well, maybe I will be done by then", and he winked at Miranda. "You know Hugh, my daughter thinks the world of you" Miranda casually said.

"Oh really, I didn't notice" Hugh answered her.

Miranda laughed and went into the kitchen Hugh followed her to get the list of what to do. "You see these?" Miranda was holding up a bag of Fritos.

"Oh yeah, I know about Fritos, my Mom buys them too."

"My daughter is a sucker for them, if you have a bag it's like a magnet for her."

"Oh, really?" Hugh said.

"Yes and if you plan on going to the skating party, I am sure if you had a bag of Fritos, my daughter would find you somehow, and sit beside you until the very last one of those Fritos were gone."

"Well I better get a pretty big bag then" Hugh said laughing.

"Oh and Hugh, April loves tuna sandwiches too", "I do too" he said.

As Hugh worked outside, the wind blew but he did not mind, his mind was elsewhere, now he was making plans to go to the skating party and he would ask his Mom for some help.

He wanted her to help him make tuna sub sandwiches and get a big bag of Fritos chips.

He wanted to get April's attention and keep it. Hugh was soon done and in the kitchen again when there was noise outside. Miranda looked out, "Oh they are back" and she reached for her jacket and went out. Hugh was behind her. Both of them helped young girls and boys tie their ponies to the rail.

Soon parents began to arrive to pick up their sons or daughters, and within fifteen minutes all of them were gone. April had begun to turn the ponies out to the dry lot and was giving them hay.

"Do you want me to fill up the water tubs for you April?" Hugh asked her. "Oh yes, that would be nice" she replied.

After the ponies were taken care of, Hugh bumped into April intentionally asking her, "So, are you planning on going to the ice skating party this coming week?"

April looked at Hugh, "I am planning on going, are you? She asked.

"I would not miss it for anything" he said laughing.

"Can you can skate?" April asked him.

"A little bit, you might have to show me", he said teasingly.

April slugged his arm lightly. They both began to laugh and they sat up on the porch swing. As they sat there Miranda watched them, "If only" she loved Hugh like a son, and well, if it were her wish these two would be together some day.

Mrs. Marshall felt as Miranda did, and quite accidently blurted it out, apologizing to Miranda. Miranda began to laugh and hugged Mrs. Marshall. "Don't apologize I am in agreement with you." And they both laughed and hugged one another.

The two kids sat there on the swing together, talking and laughing, sometimes making hand gestures. Hugh squeezed April's neck and she leaned herself against him and he put his arm around her.

Miranda held her breath. In an instant April stood up and said, "It must be three and I know I have to go milking. "I am sorry but I have to go." And she was right, she did have to go. And on this day, Miranda was in complete agreement that this was not what she wanted for her daughter either.

Here was a good opportunity for the two of these kids to get to know one another, but milking got in the way. Miranda sighed and asked Hugh to come in to be paid. He waived his hand as in "forget it" headed out to get in his truck. Hugh looked around and he soon saw April. She was headed out on the 4 wheeler. She waved to him and he waved back, and soon they both were on their way.

That following week Hugh asked his Mom for help. She was thrilled. She knew to keep it a secret. She and Miranda would talk at the ice skating event. Hugh was irritated he wanted to find "his" ice skates, and decent clothes, which was funny to his Mom.

Thursday came fast to April. The men were already at the pond the water was frozen thanks to some machinery help. The barrels were full of kindling with good fires in them for warmth. There were wooden logs for seating, and a pick-up truck would be nearby for snacks and food.

Hugh came on time, April of course was late. The milking held her back. By the time April came many kids were skating or sitting talking.

April came to the edge of the pond clumsy she had her skates on. She stepped over the edge and began to lift off, and skate.

Hugh spotted her, "Hey can you teach me to do that" he called to her. April looked around and when she saw Hugh she said, "Sure."

April skated up to Hugh and reached for his two hands to hers, grasping them. She pulled and he was a little off balance. As they began to skate Hugh began to get better, and better. By the third time around Hugh turned backwards and was skating, pulling April along.

He knew how to skate very well, and he was laughing at her. She laughed too, it was a good joke.

"Phew, I need a brake" he said, "Would you like something to drink" he asked April.

"Yes, I would like something, well anything really", and she wanted to help. "Ok you get us something to drink and I'll get the snacks" Hugh said, he was laughing to himself.

April went to the pick-up truck and asked for ginger ale with ice, please. Two large cups and she headed to the log seats. Hugh was already there. "So what do you have," she asked him.

"Hum, let me see, oh here it is, Tuna subs and Fritos," Hugh said.

He could see April perk up immediately.

"Oh, you have Fritos?" She asked.

They sat there talking about the ice party, what they were doing over the winter, and then April mentioned about the Olympics. Hugh was very interested. "Man you are lucky, I would love to go, you can be sure I will be watching you and cheering for you, we all will be" he said.

April was quiet about it all. She did not want many to know, not just yet. She had a lot of training to do. She did not want to disappoint anyone. "You, disappoint anyone? You have got to be pulling my leg, April you could do wrong, and it would still come out ok" Hugh said. "That is not true and you know it" April said. "Being the Sheriffs daughter I have to be especially good, you know what I mean" she said. "I do, but I know your parents love you very much and you are lucky for that" Hugh said to her.

"I know, don't think I don't appreciate them and all they do for me, in fact I am sad sometimes that so many things take me away from them. "But they are always encourage me to do more" April said.

Huge put what he had been eating away, began to roll up the Frito bag. April said, "What are you doing?"

"Putting it away" Hugh said.

"Why?" April said. "Because I am done with them", Hugh said.

"Well, I am not", April said.

Hugh took them and shoved off onto the ice with April in pursuit.

They were laughing and chasing each other when some other girls called them immature.

Soon they were both away from the group on the far end of the pond. April was munching, both of them talking. A very light snow began to fall and it was perfect. This moment in time was the first time in April's life she felt loved by someone other than her own family. It was as if they had known each other since the beginning of time. It all came so easy. Hugh looked at her and she at him, she was not afraid. He made her feel safe. Yes, this moment in time was one she would treasure.

For all the days of her life, she was happy.

Hugh leaned in and kissed her lips so tenderly, April closed her eyes. She was lost somewhere very pleasant, and it was over before she could think. Hugh looked at her and smiled.

Granted, no one young can or should decide on the one person they want to be with for the rest of their life. Life can change people. There are so many distractions and changes that come into young people's lives. One hundred years ago there were arranged marriages, and preteens that made lifetime commitments. However they had the support of both families all around them. And there were far, far less distractions and choices.

So the love that these two felt, would have been called, "Puppy love." they could not act on it, because of the respect they had for each other and their families. The both were raised with ethics, moral standards, and respect.

All too soon it was 9:00 p. m. and the party organizers began to call the kids in to end their activity. Adults put out the fire barrels and gathered everyone together to take back to the chapel or here for parents to pick them up.

Hugh and April skated back and as they sat together they took their skates off. Hugh was finished before April he leaded forward and kissed her cheek. April turned to say something, but he was already standing and walking up the hill to his Mother's car, where she and Mrs. Di Angelo were standing side by side together. The both looked at each other. That moment was not missed, and Miranda said, "The Frito's must have worked" and they both laughed. "Come on April" her Mother called after her.

"Mom I don't have shoes, so I am coming in my sock feet" she answered her.

"So much for womanly forethought" Miranda said to herself.

Yes, April was an outstanding, athletic, caring, kind, exemplary young woman. But there were times that she had an empty head, or so her Mother thought.

"On the way home April began to yawn, coming in from the cold, into the warm car, she began to fight sleep.

"The reason you are sleepy, it is almost 9:30 p.m. your bedtime. You know morning comes very early for you, so it's home, change, shower and bed for you my Sweet girl.

April said nothing she knew her Mom was right. She had left her boots in the car. She had put her skates on in the car, so of course she did not have her boots to change in to at the pond. April did not blame her Mom and she was not angry with her either. Her Mom did so much for her and from time to time April felt she deserved to be lectured. April was not an adult her Mom was. April hated to see kids argue with their parents, it was disrespectful.

Every day, the alarm went off at 3:45 a.m. she yawned, got up, went into the bathroom. Dragged her clothes down stairs, got dressed, some hot cocoa, and out the door, to start am milking by 4 or 4 10 am. Then it was hurry up to feed the calves at various places and home to give the ponies care and feed. If she was lucky she could have breakfast with Dad. If not she usually got to kiss him good bye. April would then take off her barn clothes, shower and get ready for school. For now she did not ride Native Son. And some days she missed it.

But today April was exhausted. It was nice knowing Native Son was rested, she needed more.

As she walked to the school bus stopped she could see the bus coming from far in the distance, away on the other hill side. Soon it would dip down and be gone to reappear to their upside and level on their road.

Winter Olympics

BOY, SHE THOUGHT, I MIGHT BE LEAVING AGAIN, AND SOON. I NEED to remember to talk to Dad tonight about that woman Gail and hear my parent's thoughts on the winter Olympics. In a way it would be a good time to go. I know Beth would cover for me in the milking and Native Son is in breeding. It really is just the ponies and calves care. Well, it's up to them. But I think I would like to go. And with that the bus came rumbling along and April got on.

As a reminder she wrote Olympics on the folder top to see it when she got home. She was doing homework when Dad came home and Mom was almost finished with dinner. April took her books and papers off of the table and began to set the table. As they all sat together, April brought up the subject of the winter games, to hear what her parent's thoughts were.

The conversation was light and easy, it was obvious Mom and Dad both had thought it thought it out, if she wanted to go, she could and they were in full support of her, they already had some help enlisted. April sat there confused.

She did not expect this but she knew with the last Olympics her parents were proud and very happy about it. This should be no different. But April knew it would definitely be different for her. It would take a lot of her time, stamina, strength and mental strength to win. April wanted to talk to her parents about this and Gordon stood up and made a phone call, "Ok, you are? That's great, see you in ten minutes" he hung up the phone and winked at his wife.

Sure enough in ten minutes in walked Judge Du Val, who sat down for dinner and have a talk with April. After dinner he escorted April into the parlor room and they had a hard long talk. April needed this. She needed a sounding board. To talk to someone just how she felt, no holding back. April cried, she laughed, shook her head yes and no. She realized what a great mentor the Judge was for her and so very grateful for his friendship.

After their talk, April stood up with tears in her eyes to thank him. The Judge stood up and hugged her in a great big bear hug. "I am here for you, whenever you need to talk, just ask me" he said "anytime!"

As they came out of the parlor both Gordon and Miranda were standing near the door entry, both saying, "Well?" and the Judge put up his right thumb. Gordon reached for his daughter pulling her to him he could no longer lift her up in his arms. At that same moment Mom's arms were around her as well. They were crying tears of joy.

With a huge sigh of relief and a little anxiety both Gordon and Miranda stepped back.

Gordon said, "I will call Gail to come over this week, we need to sign papers, and give money again" and they laughed.

"Are you sure, are you really sure you can take care of things, because this time is going to be much harder" April said to them. "Yes we know, we have both discussed this many, many times, and feel this challenge will be good for you, to test your strength, your skills, so we are sure".

April went to bed that night, thinking and thinking, Ruby was beside her lying so still, but watching her with her big round eyes.

April pet Ruby's head and said, "Sure, all you want is me here with you, like everyone else, but you sure say way less" and she ruffled her fur. As April slept she was skiing down mountain sides, and laughing, with the wind in her hair, the snow stinging her face, she remembered snow, and she liked it. She slept with a smile on her face.

And that is how it happened. In late November April was on an airplane to Poland. April's luggage was minimal she had five days change of clothing, that was it, mostly pants and shirts, nothing fancy and a plain pull over dress for church on Sundays, one, just one. Her Mom and Dad said with her staying there with a family and training she would either dress simple as the farmers did, and buy some clothing there. April personally was relieved she was not a big clothing girl. She loved her jeans and sneakers she dressed out of respect for God and Jesus Christ to go to church. Many would tell her, dress for success, but on the back of Native Son she wore what everyone else did. Jockey silks, and no one could tell them apart other than color.

On To Poland

THE FLIGHT WAS A LONG ONE. APRIL SAT IN THE ECONOMY SECTION. April was not afraid of flying she had flown with Native Son on one trip into Los Angeles California. She remembered seeing all the casinos lit up and all of the housing lights in a straight line row.

April did take a book along it was something for her to do. Instead she pulled out some paper and a pen and began to write a letter to her parents, some habits never change. She often tapped the pen against her lips as she searched for words to adequately express how she felt.

It only took her a half hour to write to them and she carefully folded the letter, put it in an onion skin envelope. She addressed it and carefully put it in her back pack she carried with her. April wanted to be sure to mail it as soon as she got off of the plane. April sat there watching the many passengers. There were older people, young people with young children. Some were students, she guessed. Many were business travelers.

When someone tapped April lightly on her shoulder "Excuse me", said the stewardess, "Are you the girl who rides the famous race horse?" April answered her. "Yes, I am, but I also own him, Native Son is my horse."

"I see" she said. "It was of great interest here in our country that such a young person such as yourself had the talent and strength to train and ride such a fine animal". April said, "I raised him from a baby so he thinks I am his Mom. I love him and I am pretty sure he loves me. We bonded so we both have learned to listen to each other."

"The girls and I were talking when we first saw you enter the plane and three of us believed it was you" she said.

She then waved her hand and the other girls came to where April was sitting. "Hello" they all said in good English. They each said their names but for the life of her, April could not remember them or pronounce them from memory. They remarked at how fast Native Son could run, like he had a double speed inside him. April agreed with them she said he was so much fun to ride. "Are you not afraid?" one asked her. "No, April said, "I love it."

"Were you not in the Olympics a while back riding the famous Roger?" one asked her. "Yes I was, that was my first Olympics and Roger was a sturdy mount, very talented and strong."

"What brings you to Poland to grace us?" the shy girl asked. "I am entering the winter Olympics. I begin my training when I touch down." April answered her. "Oh, then we will watch for you and cheer for you." she said excitedly and they all were nodding their heads yes. It was a lovely visit they were very kind to April. Later they brought April her favorite treat, a hot chocolate with tiny marsh mellows and crackers.

Touch down and April waited for most of the passengers to disembark from the airplane. She did not understand what was being said on the loud speaker. April had a sign she remembered to place around her neck. She pulled it out of her backpack and hung it around her neck. She felt a bit silly, but knew it was the only way the person waiting there to pick her up would find her. As she stood up one of the stewardess, squeezed her arm, saying "Good Luck"

April smiled at her, "To you too" and she turned to go.

Out of the plane down a small enclosed plank into the airport terminal, she watched for the person to pick her up, she saw no one. So she went to the baggage claim and picked up her one suitcase and waited.

Then April noticed short statured man. He was in his 50's with a grey mustache and a hat. He approached her but he did not know much English. She did not know Polish. He had on a grey sweater and jodhpurs, and muck boots. He had short stubby strong hands, and she did not know what he said, but his sign matched hers. It was ok, she thought.

April saw a female guard on the way out and asked the woman kindly if she would mind mailing the letter she had written to her parents. She handed the woman a five dollar American bill and the woman smiled and took the letter and the money.

The man took April's suitcase, and put it in the back of a small pick-up truck, and held the driver's side door open for her to get in. That was the driver's side in the United States. But here, that was the passenger side. Here in the drivers drove on the right. April smiled at him, got in and he closed the door. The man got in on the left side which was the passenger side in the U.S. He started the engine and they were off. The truck was bumpy and they drove very fast across the highways and made their way to the country side.

It was a two hour ride to reach the family where April would be staying. They seemed like a nice family, two boys and a girl, Mom & Dad. There was Anna Maria the Mother, Hajinko, the Father.

Then their children, Anna Marinka the daughter and Hal and Peter their sons. They were the hopeful future Olympians. The boys were speed skaters the boys were tall and lanky, and very shy.

April enjoyed Mrinka very much Mousy, as her family fondly called her was a soft spoken young woman with big round loving eyes. Together those two milked goats, shoveled snow, walked to school and skated.

The boys were rough. They challenged April at every step. They were stronger and faster than April was, in the beginning. Their father Hajinko, was their coach and he helped April immensely in bringing her around to be ready for the Olympics.

Hajinko had injured his shoulder recently and could not milk the goats he was willing to train April in her events "if" she could help provide a support for their family. April was more than willing and able, that is why she was paired with this family.

The goats were Toggenburg's. They were native to this country they were popular in the USA as well. They were small good natured animals, easy to work with and these in particular were well trained. Every a.m. and every p.m. the goats would line up and begin their march, one by one, in a line into the small milking parlor. They walked up planks, and each would put their head thru a small stanchion, on an elevated floor. They stood until they were finished being milked and then would step back two steps, turn to the right slightly and walk back outside, to rejoin their herd.

It was quite amazing to see these little creatures, know their jobs so well.

April was impressed, if only everyone did their job as well, as these goats did, without complaining. But boy oh boy, they sure like getting paid. April knew that some people only came to work to collect a paycheck.

This was April's daily routine, every a.m. and every p.m., during the day is when she trained, under the watchful eye of Hajinko. Who they all called Jinks for short. Jinks started April with running. She was expected to run two miles in under 10 minutes. Each day cut her time down. April then ran with weights strapped to her ankles, wrists and biceps, it was not easy for her to swing her arms.

After April was used to those weights, Jinks added weights to April's shoulders. In all she was running with 60 additional pounds. It was difficult at first, but soon became part of her. In fact without weights on, with regular walking became difficult, April over walked, and became off balance without the weights. Often she took someone's hand to steady her, and they all understood.

Jinks had been a phenomenal, ski racer when he was young. He had medals galore. He was going to teach April all he knew about ski racing. His own sons chose not to ski race, the wanted to skate race.

April practiced all hours, in the early morning before milking, in the afternoon and in the evenings after milking. She also helped with bailing of hay, stacking it in their barn. It was something she was familiar with, having helped at home. April shocked wheat, and made corn rows in stacks, it was an efficient way to store them without using a building.

Yes, life here was not much different than at home, she did of course miss her home and her parents. April wrote faithfully to her parents to let them know how she was, and what she was doing. The Mother of the Polish family, Anna Maria was quite impressed. She had read some of the letters April's wrote and she was touched with what April's words said, in conveying the love she had for her parents and the Polish family. Yes, Anna Maria was starting to love this young girl as if she were theirs. She could not help it. It was not like she had a button to turn off. One evening she called her daughter Miranka to her side to speak to her about this.

Miranka was not jealous at all, she herself felt as if April had always been there, she fit right in. April never balked at work, and did more than her share. Miranka loved it when she and April would go to town and buy material. April always had good ideas on how to make a plain dress pretty, using additional material or simple beads. Miranka also loved it when April would put up her hair in braids, with ribbons. Miranka did not have a sister, but April called her sister all the time. They enjoyed one another's company. They could be goofy together, talk about boys, or animals, it was so easy to be with her. Miranka knew when April left she was going to miss her immensely. She pushed those thoughts aside and reassured her Mother she was fine with it all, because she loved April too. Anna Maria was pleased.

The boys were a different story that played out on its own. Both Hal and Peter began to make competition to show off in front of April, but she did not care. April saw them and both her and Miranka called the boys fools. To which the Father Jinks and Mother Anna agreed.

The three of them had training, running, more training and eating right for Hal, Peter and April. There were no more baked goodies for the three of them. It was no hardship for April she did not like candy at all. But the baked goods from Anna Maria's oven were overpoweringly delicious smelling. April would leave the room or go outside to escape the delicious smells. The boys would sneak food, but were caught by Jinks and always, had to do laps.

So daily they ice skated while April skied alongside of them, it was always a race and they would laugh at each other, as if racing was a surprise! By the two month mark April was able to overtake the boys in races. The muscles in her legs, back and arms were powerfully strong. April did not tire easily anymore. She relished racing and loved especially the surprise of impromptu races.

Day after day, each day was added on more or longer skills to do. April never complained. Just pitch in and do it, get it done, was April's attitude. Jenks was impressed with her, she listened, she followed thru, if she had a question, she asked. She was easy to train, she was obedient. Not like the boys, especially Peter, who balked and questioned everything.

As the months went by, Jenks arm was not as sore and he joined in the barn for milking. It was obvious the goats missed him, one by one as they come in they all pressed their tiny noses into his hands as he lovingly, softly spoke to them. Yes, these were beasts of burden, but also lovingly treated as pets.

All too soon it was time to be ready for the Olympics. Each day of the month was crossed off of the calendar.

Each month flipped back around to the back of the calendar. The Olympic week was circled in red, as a stark reminder.

They were ready, all three of them. The boys and April had worked hard, played hard, trained everyday as they teased one another. They encouraged one another. They were in every sense a team, a family. As the days went by Hal and Peter became nervous, they were undecided at small tasks their minds were long gone from the farm, although their feet were still on the farm. April wanted to do the task at hand, they would be at the Olympics soon enough, and now mattered.

One evening as they had supper of kale soup, the father Jinks wanted to talk to the children. Momma Anna brought come cinnamon tea for the three of them. Jinks explained that they did all they could to be prepared, but all that happens there, he could not prepare them.

He wanted his boys to stay together. Jinks was going along to their events. But for April he encouraged her to find someone in common with her, and if she could not, stay apart, but strong inside. He assured April her coach would be there, and there were other girls. But he felt strongly she would be alright. April had came a long way to train and did not know them ahead of time. She showed strength, trust and put her best foot forward at all times. He placed his strong hands on her shoulders, and said, "I will be watching you, cheering for you, we all will." "You can win, I know it, I feel it inside, here" he said as he touched his chest. "You have heart, you big strength inside you, I feel it, I have seen it". He kissed April on her forehead and hugged her.

That was something, really something for April. She never felt that she deserved such a great place to stay, and be taught so much.

April responded to Jinks, and said, "I am grateful for your time and experience you have shared with me. I, I'm almost speechless. I promise you that I will do my best, and not shirk or take a back seat.

I have come to train with the best and I have come to win, I will not let you down."

That night as she lay in bed, across from Miranka, she whispered, "Are you asleep" Miranka answered she was not.

April got up from her bed and sat beside Miranka. April reached over to hug her and found Miranka was crying.

April felt bad, so she got up and carefully moved her bed beside her friend. She spoke to her and said. "Don't cry, it's going to be alright."

Miranka could not answer her she just nodded her head. April was not going to leave her. Their beds were side by side touching. April got in and in the morning the Mother found them with their arms across on each other's bed.

Winter Olympics

It was a confusing time, but one April grabbed on to and held on tight. It was challenging and she liked a challenge.

The winter park was huge! There were people and buildings everywhere. Each sport had its own areas and the competitors in those sports were housed near those complexes.

April was driven to a housing place and the check point confirmed where she was to be. She got out of the car and began to unload her bags.

April understood she was in two, possibly three events.

1. Ski sharp shooting, 2. Ski racing, only If they needed her she was willing to participate in the Ski Jump. April was ready, she had practiced for months. She had been injured, sore, bruised, worked out, ran for miles and miles every day. Strength trained, ate well, she was healthy and strong, both physically and mentally. April trusted Jinks and had every intention to follow his well thought out advice for her.

As she checked in to her hotel she was assigned a room, there were three other girls with her in the same room. They were on the Ski team as well, but she did not know them because she had not trained with them.

April lugged her two bags with her up to the lobby onto the stairs. The main room was full, she must have said "excuse me, pardon me" twenty times.

At the stairs she began to step to the top. From the top at the rail she could see the entire vast room. There were wooden beams all around her. Thick beams on the ceiling were awesome.

There were huge windows that offered view to what was going on outside. The room was very warm, even with the open space and windows. The temperature outside was sixteen degrees, but not cold to her. April had gotten used to the cold having worked, trained and lived with the family she had been assigned to and whom she learned to love.

April did not see the boys. Of course would be near the speed skating rink. But she was sure she would see them at some point, she hoped so anyway. She wanted to cheer for them as they were like a second family to her. It was hard to believe it was December here. There was snow, snow, snow everywhere.

She walked to the door that had the number 14 on it. She inserted the credit card key into the slot, slid the card down and the door opened automatically.

She stepped inside and there were three girls sitting on one bed looking at photos.

April instinctively said "Hello" the girls looked up but said nothing, one girl waved a hello. April lugged her bags inside, placing one at the widow side bed. "Excuse me that is my bed" one girl said to her.

"Awesome" April replied, which one is mine?"

The girl pointed to the door, "I don't think so" April said and she placed her bag on the bed by the window.

She walked to the girls, out stretching her hand saying, "My name is April D. I am in three different events and I am not going to put up with bullying, gossip or plain wasting time. We can be kind and friendly to one another, or rude. The choice is yours." and she went and sat on her bed. She began to take out her necessary things, such as tooth brush, combs and so on. When the two girls came over to her bed and sat down.

"Hi my name is Ivy, and this is Ruth" Ivy said. "I am very glad to meet you both" April replied. The other girl sat on the opposite bed, looking at pictures.

"Don't mind her, that's Melissa, she is a moody girl all the time anyway." Ivy said laughing, and that is when Melissa thru a pillow at Ivy. April caught the pillow in midair and lobbed it back at Melissa, hitting her in the head.

"Hey, watch it" Melissa said.

"No, YOU watch it" April told her. "You have a bad attitude and a bad attitude is like a flat tire, you won't go far like that." The two girls giggled and Melissa huffed.

The girls were in the Louge-race. They would run pushing a bullet shaped sled, hop in one at a time as fast as they could. Their heads forward and one girl would steer going 85 mph or faster to the finish line. "Wow, that's really something" April said. "I would love to see you race and learn about it, honest I am impressed" and the two girls giggled. They were first time runners, very excited and very nervous.

Soon there was a knock on their door. Melissa got up to open the door and April thru a pillow at her. "Don't do that, you don't know who is on the other side." 'It may be a coach, it may not be, it may be a robber. You don't know." April got up and stood in front of the door. "Who is it?" she asked. "I have the pizza you ordered," the voice said. April looked back at the girls who were all shaking their heads NO.

April knocked on the door, and said, "You have the wrong room we are allergic to tomato sauce." "Come on, don't give me bull" the voice said. "Ok, no bull, get lost, go find the right room and don't bother us again you jerk" April said sternly. And with that the voice disappeared.

April went back to the bed and sat down. The two girls Ivy and Ruth were upset, but April quickly put them to ease, "Let's play a game ok?" "Let's practice what you do, you girls can use the bathtub." They got up and began to show April how they did their run, even Melissa joined them. They began to focus and concentrate and it was all work in that tub.

Soon another knock came on their door, only this time it was their coach. She identified herself, and called their names out. They opened their door. She was impressed they were practicing in the tub. She laid out food vouchers and some other things for the girls to do. She cautioned them to stay together, not to leave the complex. April assured her they would be alright. She eyed April closely she did not really know her and was a bit standoffish.

April explained she was the one who trained with the Polish family for her sport event. And all at once, as if a light went off in her brain her eyes brightened and she said, "Oh yes, now I know" and that was that.

The girls began to grab the food vouchers and Ruth was able to stop them. She divided them up equally. This way they could trade for other things. Be it souvenirs' or other things like, well, just about anything.

They decided to go to the food court and order and then get some practice in. So they all left their room, locking the door and headed to the food court together. They were confused at some of the menu choices. April decided to eat what they had there, culturally experience the food. And then she laughed to herself. They had polish sausage with peppers and onions and perogie's. April loved, loved perogie's. So life at the food court was good!

The girls all sat together at one table, some did not like their food choices and wanted perogie's too. All of a sudden April saw a familiar face and got up to run to hug her friend. There was Miranka aka Mousy. They both hugged each other while Anna Marie stood by with tears.

They soon were at the table with April in a flurry of talking and laughing. April did not want to be rude. She introduced the girls to her friends who were more like family to her All too soon they had to leave. They hugged both of her friends, Mother and daughter and left with the girls for the night

Once in their rooms they all began to settle down. Thankfully since all of them had trained for a sport they were all tired at night. They were used to a routine it was lights out at 8:30 p.m.

April was asleep fast, as were the other three girls.

As usual April was up early at 4 a.m. dressed and wanted to go for a run. As she locked her room door and went down the stairs. April noticed another person by a door. April looked directly at this person it was a girl, who had strong features. She was built like a rock, but she was extremely nice and friendly. She too wanted to go out for a run. They decided to stay together for safety, it was a fantastic run and they challenged one another.

They were not winded or tired, the fresh crisp air suited them both. They decided to build a snow man in front of their building. That snowman ended up fourteen foot tall, holding on to a bobsled, complete with scarf, hat and a carrot nose.

Many commented on the snowman, they all loved it. They had pictures taken in front or with the snow man posing. April and the two girl high fived each other for the good job they did. Then they headed back to their own rooms to rejoin their groups. As April entered the room, no one was inside. She sat on her bed with a pen and paper and wrote another letter to her parents and to the woman who had made her winter hat.

It was from the grocery folks, the Rex's who had been so kind to her when she was lost. They stopped by one afternoon, and dropped it off for April.

Her hat was knitted and lovingly made with red white and blue around the cap it also had a spray of knit string and at the very top, with red white and blue sprigs all going in different directions as April ran, walked or when the wind blew.

April concentrated on the letter and was finished in no time she folded it and put it in onion skin envelopes she had purchased before coming back to the room.

She began to be sleepy and snuggled into a soft chair that was in the room. She covered up with one of her blankets and in no time was dozing off.

She woke with a start as she heard a knock on their door. It was the girls they did not have their card key to come into the room. As she got up and opened the door, the girls came bounding in along with one of the coaches.

She introduced herself, Romaine Salisa. She was the coach for the speed ski and shoot competition. She was also part time coach for the speed ski team. She was small woman with an athletic body. She was soft spoken and difficult to hear. She motioned for April to follow her, so April did.

They walked down the stairs to the ground floor out to another stadium building. Inside there were all sort of guns and rifles for the ski, shoot and ski competition.

Romaine showed April the gun she was to use she said it was possible to make modifications if April knew what she wanted. Having shot guns with her Dad, April understood what the coach was telling her. She hoisted up one of the rifles and held it to her shoulder, scoping thru the site, then she put it down. "Nope, that one is too heavy" she said.

She went thru several of them and settled for a medium weight with a snub nose. She liked this one because at home she had a 243 snub rifle that she used to ground hog hunt. A groundhog can make tunnels and holes that when a hay wagon goes across, the wagon will tilt and often sink in and tip over. That is why she hunted ground hogs in the summer time on their hay fields and the 243 was super at shooting at 300 yards. "I will have our guys look at this gun for you, to make sure this is the right one for you" Romaine said.

She then took April to the uniforms. There were red white and blue uniforms like coveralls, only tighter fit and very light, with mostly white. The colors were on the chest, wrists and leggings and these were this year's colors. April was impressed, snow and white, USA colors showed but they were not showy or loud. It was beginning to feel real to April. They headed out to look for skis. Romaine explained to April she should be practicing to stay in shape for the race in the next two days.

Two days were like nothing, in no time it would be the day. April asked about what the limitations were for her. Could she run during the day and where. Could she ski whenever she wanted for distance and where was she allowed to go.

Romaine answered all the questions for April. Basically she could run whenever she wanted on the track. It was safe, well lighted and to ski the same place.

Granted it was going around in a circle but it was safe and would certainly give a good work out. Romaine reminded April there was official practice at 7 a.m. starting tomorrow. If she chose to practice in the afternoon, that was April's choice.

April wanted to practice right now! This day and then because she was usually up early at 4 a.m. she thought she could get some practice in before the "practice" with the team. That is what she decided.

She found a good pair of skis and began to free ski on the track. She took it easy at first setting her own pace to a song she had in her head. And then after ten minutes she decided to push herself a little more and go faster for about twenty laps.

Her mind was in a song that was very fast beat and tempo. Not long after she began to ski she found some spectators watching her. One was a photographer, and then there were other athletes who was just relaxing.

She kept on and soon she was joined by two others, it was Peter and Hal, and that made her smile from ear to ear.

They did not let on they knew her and she knew why.

They were on different levels, from different countries and it was out of respect. She did however challenge them on the ski track and it was not hard for her to do. She was now well seasoned and great shape. She kept up with them and felt she could pass them at any time. But she did not, she wanted to keep some surprises intact.

April left the tract after her work out, waving to the two men skiers, who waved back. She entered her room and found the girls gone. She thought they were taken by their coach to practice their sport of Louge-run.

April decided since she did not have breakfast she should eat something so she headed to the food court. She saw some egg omelettes in a wrap with vegetables. She got that and some orange juice, took her tray to a table and sat down. As she was eating, she suddenly had hands over her eyes and someone saying "Can you guess who this is?" April did not know, she wanted them to say more to guess by their voice but they were silent. When the hands were removed April was surprised and speechless. It was her parents, Gordon and Miranda, and her Grandparents, Manny (Poppo) and Contessa.

They had all come. April was so overwhelmed with happiness she began to cry. She was so happy they were here with her.

She hugged them all and in a short while they were walking towards April's house and room. Once inside there was little room to sit and talk. There was a lot to talk about. It was obvious to Miranda that April was nervous, her mind was elsewhere. She knew that their presence there at the games to support April was a great source of comfort. But she had to concentrate on what she was here for, not to visit but to do well in her events.

April asked how everything was at home and Gordon explained that the animals were in good hands. They just had to come. Manny said wild horses could not have kept him from coming and he winked at her. They left soon to allow April time to think and concentrate. After they left April began to make plans for her events. She laid out her clothes for an evening run and sure enough when she went out the girl she had met the previous day was there. The two of them ran like there was a tiger chasing after them. They ran hard and it was good. It made them tired, a good tired, to be able to sleep to be fresh in the morning Practice! Practice makes perfect. But then there are things that happen, a fall, overconfidence or under confidence, many things can come into play to change the whole situation.

April pushed herself to keep a steady pace. Not to go all out. She was not a favorite but that was fine with her. She knew that as the race began nerves would take a large part and she would get strength from adrenaline.

That day after practice she ran for two hours in the afternoon, had lunch, waited a ½ hour and ran again. She ran two hours before the p.m. practice and after it as well. This was her routine for the two days before her event.

On her race day the ski and shoot completion was her first event. April was 15th out of the gate. April knew she had to have a fast time and be accurate. She had that song with the fast tempo in her head and pushed off. At her first stop April missed one shot and was allowed a 2nd shot. She got it and did a double time, passing the leader. On the second round she was in first. April did not miss any of her shots. She slung her gun over her shoulder with ski poles in each hand and pushed of hard. She pushed herself harder than when she trained with Jinks.

They went around ten times, and as she came down the hill for the last time, she knew she was in the lead.

The women from Germany and Poland were visibly tired. You could hear them breathing hard. April was as too but not as much as they were. She knew it was due to the conditioning

Jenks had her do and she was faithful in keeping with what he taught her.

As she skied down the last small hill the side line of people were yelling and screaming, she did not see anyone in particular yet she knew her family was there. As she crossed the finish line she felt relieved, tired and wanted to get a drink of something cold.

When all at once she felt arms around her, it was her Dad and Manny. They had come from the side lines and were there for her. It was her Mom and Contessa they wanted to congratulate April as well. Mom had tears in her eyes, and April wiped them away with her hands. "It's ok Mom, really it is" April said to her. "I know dear, I am just so proud of you" her Mom said. Contessa held her hands to April's face and kissed her forehead she too had tears she told April they were tears of joy.

That event was over, now April had two days of working out for the twenty mile ski race. She did not want to think of it right now, not this day!

That evening her family took her out to eat. It was a swanky restaurant, with a band playing. The songs were good, really good. April began to dance as she ate sweet potato fries.

Her Dad told her to go out on the floor and dance. April looked at him incredibly like he was crazy. She did not have a dance partner. "You go out and dance and you will get a partner" her Dad said. So she did, and her Dad was right. There were two boys who joined her on the floor and it was a lot of fun. Neither of the boys could speak English and April had no clue what they were saying. But it was ok, they all had a great time, it was a great stress reliever.

Afterwards they all headed out. They dropped April at her place and continued on to their hotel. At the hotel where Gordon and Miranda shared a room with Manny and Contessa they all talked about April and her upcoming race. As much as they wanted to be with her, they understood April had to prepare this next race was a long hard race. Up hills, along roads, past woods, and highways, around small set up courses and around again, it was very challenging. At night they found themselves playing Uno or some other games Mom had brought along.

They all headed to bed early, soon Manny and Contessa were snoring, and Gordon and Miranda talked. Gordon held Miranda's head in the crook of his arm as they lay in bed.

He felt his wife's tears on his arm, "Don't cry sweetheart" he said to his wife softly. "I know, I know but she is only fourteen and doing such big things, and I love her so much" Miranda said

Gordon tapped her arm, "I know you do, but I think our daughter is like a small dog. The dog does not know it is small. So it goes out and has all the adventures it wants, afraid of nothing."

Miranda laughed and sniffled. "Our daughter is not a dog" she said.

"I know she is not" Gordon teasingly squeezed her to him, but she is not afraid and that is so good. She is open to almost anything. She will give all of 100 percent of herself. We have seen it at home with the ponies, and in everything she does."

"You're right" Miranda said. "I am just worried about tomorrow. It is such a long race, and the weather is concerning me. They are watching the storm closely. They are not sure if they will have the race or postpone it. If they postpone it that will throw off their schedule, so I just don't know" she said. "Well there is little we can do about the weather you know that, so let's just see how this plays out." With that he kissed his wife and hugged her and they slept just like that.

The next day April was gone, either running or skiing. She was joined by several other women who were in the twenty mile. April stayed away from them. She did not want to be unfriendly but she was not here to make friends. Not before the race. After the race was a different time.

April practiced skiing, running and keeping in tune with an inner voice that kept her going. By night fall she knew she had to sleep but her mind would not rest. She had a for-boding feeling so she got out of her bed, on her knees and offered a prayer. She asked God to help her, to calm her down, to allow her to get the rest she needed for the race and what was to come. She asked for help to do her best, to please him. To show by example. April asked for his grace and his mercy. Then she crawled into bed and didn't remember a thing, she was out.

That morning she was up and awake at 4 a. m. as usual. She was ready, mentally, physically and emotionally. She got up and dressed. The girl's event was later that day and they were still asleep. April slipped out of the room, not to wake them. She went down the stairs and felt she should eat something. The food court was just beginning to cook. She saw a man that came out, and he winked at her, then he disappeared. He came out with a cheese omelet in a wrap with orange juice container. "He remembered", she thought to herself. And then he said, "Ski well" winking at her. So he knew. April realized, so he knew.

Well that was her intention, to ski well. She waved to him and was gone.

The race was almost called, it had been a very heavily overcast morning, but about 8:00 a.m. the sun was beginning to come out. April was in her uniform, skis on, her hat firmly tied in place. Her gloves were dangling on a snap at her side pocket. All of the women competitors were waiting.

The announcement came the race would begin in a half hour. So all of the women began to talk and walk to the starting position. Each woman had a starting place and time. April was twenty third in line. This was a timed event so it did not matter what number you were. You had to have the least amount of time to win.

At 8:30 a.m. the women all were in position, the judges were present and one was on a chair to begin the start. They all listened as the numbers were counted down, 30, 29, 28, and so on. April was ready she took her foot stance to push off. 10, 9, 8, 7, 6, 5, 4 and the people began to make yelling noises, 3, 2, 1 and the gun shot off. All of the women began to push off.

It was crazy, some were entangled with others skis, April held back a bit, and let them go she knew what she had to do.

As they headed out there was a long stretch of highway that April kept a song in her head that she used to listen to when she and the boys would skate on the water-dykes.

She was skiing along, passing a skier every now and then.

She went up hills, through the wooded areas, that were breathtaking to see. Up hills which required a lot of pushing and leg power. On to the flats, down hills, and she passed more. On to a manmade course, down and around and start over. The first time around she found herself with about twelve out in front of her. Which she thought was not bad at all.

At the third time around the course the weather began to change. The wind picked up and it began to snow. There was hail in the storm as well. Without any knowledge to the skiers the storm blew some of the skiers off course. The wind whipped up the snow making visibility very poor. The snow came fast and hard. April realized there could be trouble. She checked the landmarks she had seen before. The large stone, the tree that was crooked, the ribbon markers and made her way slowly. If she skied fast the wind would knock her down she did not want to go over the side of the steep bank.

She was not skiing fast but she was still passing skiers, some were afraid. You could see the fear on their faces. April did not want to look at them, they looked at her. She kept going.

As they went around again, they could not see, the sky was dark and the snow kept coming. Every now and then there was a gust of wind that made standing difficult.

Some would stop and hold onto something. April found that bending low helped a lot, her face hurt from the pelting of the hail. She wiped her wet cheek and saw red on her glove.

They sky was dark, the wind howled and trees began to fall. You could hear them crack and fall. As she headed into the wooded area some of the trees had fallen onto the road way where they skied. She had to go around and pick thru the logs to get past. April had almost made it when a terrible gust of wind came and blew and blew and blew, making it impossible to go anywhere. April found a walnut tree near her and she stood in front of it for protection. Some of the trees lying on the roadway were blown off of the road down over the embankment. It was frightening, but she pushed that out of her mind. She was going to be alright, she kept say that to herself.

April watched in horror as some of the women were swept off over the bank, some had held onto the trees and were gone. April did not know what to do. She could not see to rescue them. Surely someone was watching on the cameras and knew what was happening. April stood her ground beside a walnut tree.

She realized she had to get out of this area it was a dangerous place. Much more dangerous than being on the opposite hill where there were no trees to fall.

April knelt down and bowed her head in a prayer and then stood and continued on. She skied past an area where trees had been lying on the ground she saw no other skiers. On to the hills she picked her way battling the wind and the snow. The sleet pelted her face she held her breath and pushed on. She began to think of the little engine that could. And she said to herself, "I think I can, I think I can" and that is how she went.

Back in the studios there was chaos and panic. Some of the cameras were not working and those that were, showed a very grim picture. They would have a very difficult time editing this scene. And what about those who were injured or blown off of the side? Some rescue persons should go out there, but the word was the storm was too bad, they had to wait.

There were people with orange flags warning people to turn back. They put bright yellow tape across the ski way to stop skiers but there were none. As they watched thru the camera on the hill there were a few skiers who were not waiting. There were three maybe five who had made it through. They did not know who was on the course or who had fallen.

And then the cameras picked up something unusual on one of the skier's heads, it looked like a celebration spray on their head.

The top was white with bands of colors which they could not make out. Undeniably there was a springy bunch of something on the head of that one skier.

That was what the one reporter showed Gordon and Miranda who were quite worried. The video showed something bouncing on the one skier's head. Miranda's eyes flew open wide, "That her, that's our daughter, that is the hat that was made for her by the Rex family." And she praised God.

The climb to the top of the hill was a battle, every step forward felt like you went back three. Each one you had to dig in and lean forward and push. It took a lot of strength to get to the top of that hill. When she finally made it to the top she looked behind her and gasped at the sight. Half of the forest trees were down. Many people were at the bottom or on top of trees calling for help the wind was so strong it cut off cries for help.

She turned and pushed off. She just had to let the officials know. She did not want anyone to perish because of this storm. The wind was not as strong as it was in the wooded valley, so she pushed on. April again recalled a song in her head and kept a beat with her feet. On she went over small hills around curves and down to the manmade track.

April did not see anyone, but she did see bright yellow tape. She ducked under it and called for help. April hollered and called and a shovel flying in the wind nearly hit her. She thought, that's enough of that! She skied close to a camera and looked into it saying, "There has been a terrible storm. Many skiers are trapped in the wooded area. They are calling for help please help them, please!" She knew her pleas would be heard, so she continued on.

April had kept count on the laps she had made each one since the storm was treacherous. The storm was lap eleven (11) and since then she went around two (2) more times, that meant she had seven (7) more times to go around till the finish. She was beginning to feel tired, that storm really took a lot out of her. Her legs felt as if they were beginning to cramp. She did not want that. She fished a pebble out of her pocket and put it under her tongue. She knew that her body would produce more liquid if she did that. She pushed everything out of her mind and concentrated on the last seven laps. April had recognized many spots on the laps and she recalled them as she approached them, as if she were on a road map, recalling the land marks.

April knew there were other skiers out there somewhere behind her she got glimpses of a head every now and then.

Still she pushed herself on. As she rounded the pole at the start of the last lap, she saw people outside, lining up to cheer them. The storm had turned to all rain. It was a steady rain which made skiing difficult. The people called to the skiers to encourage them.

The last lap and she was really tired, but she had to finish. She knew it would be a struggle, but she was not going to quit. She HAD to keep going. April noticed two other skiers coming behind her as she edged her way up the hilly terrain. The ice made the skis slippery, hard to find and edge to stay up. But she refused to give up. On and on she went, around the rocks, up the bend, down two small hills, onto the wooded area.

She did not look but she did hear the rescue groups, some had chain saws and machinery to help them. For that she was glad. This was her race and she had to keep going. There was nothing she could do to help them. Thru the wooded area, back up another hill, onto the flat and two more hills and then a downhill to the finish line. As she was on the last hill a Chinese skier was near her, and coming behind her was another skier, she could not make out the country. As the Chinese skier came near her she could see this skier was spent and with that she collapsed on the ice. April was shocked. Her first reaction was to call to get her up.

"Get Up" April called to her she looked up and did not see the other skier. Which meant the other skier was in the down side of the 1st hill. "Get Up" April bent down slapping the ice to awaken the skier to listen. She motioned for the skier to rise with her hands.

People were beginning to line up on either side of them calling to the down skier. She put her knee up and stood and they clapped. April was standing backwards toward the track when she saw the oncoming skier who was on the top of hill one. One more hill and she'd catch up with them. "Come on, let's go" April called to the Chinese girl and April began to ski towards the finish line. The Chinese girl realized what was happening and she skied slowly, but kept going towards the finish line. April turned her head to call to her, to encourage her and with each call the Chinese girl tried harder.

They had one hill and a flat to go to the finish line and the other skier was somewhere out there coming on. April turned again to call to her and with her arms she made gestures for her to move forward, to come towards her.

April hollered for the skier to focus, pointing to her eyes. She waited for the Chinese girl and the both of them, skied down the slope onto the flat.

The Chinese girl lost her balance and fell again.

"Get Up" April screamed at her, "Get Up, you can't give in now." she pointed to the finish line. "Get Up, come on move!" The Chinese girl put her knee up and then her leg and stood and almost glided towards the finish line. April turned and skied backwards hollering at her to follow her. The other skier was coming on closer now, and they still had about ten yards to go.

"We are almost there, steady steps, and the crowds repeated what April said in their native language. April saw another Chinese girl along the side lines calling to the Chinese skier. They went on like this with eight yards to go when April skied again beside the Chinese girl, counting the steps, 1, 2, …. 1, 2, …. Just like that, and the Chinese girl smiled.

And just like that they crossed the finish line with the other skier crossing within minutes after them. The crowd erupted in shouts of joy and euphoria. They were swept up in arms and pats of congratulations. April saw her coach who was crying.

It was a bit confusing, but April felt she did the right thing it was not the most important thing to have the fastest time ever because another skier needed help. That was what was important to April.

April hoped she would not be disqualified for helping her. Soon her parents were at her side. Both of them had tears. Her Mother kept saying how proud of her she was, such a good girl. Her Dad's eyes beamed and April knew what she did was right.

At the medals ceremony it was traditional at first the three of them received their medals USA Gold, China Silver and Russia Bronze.

Then the ceremonies turned emotional, when the Chinese President stepped forward for an award for April. It was an award for her role of going beyond what she was expected to do. He gave a speech which many Chinese cried. April did not understand one word. But when he placed a key around her neck, she understood. He had given April the key to China. She was welcome there any time she wanted and would be treated as a royalty. "That" was mind blowing to April. Her parents were stunned, this was not expected. They and Manny and his wife were a bit overwhelmed. This was an awesome experience to have happened. Of course this happened largely in part because April refused to give up on the Chinese skier.

But it would not have mattered what countries skier was out there with April. She would have encouraged them to get up and keep going. Their daughter was not taught to help someone for fame or for gifts, she was taught to love everyone.

Just like Jesus Christ did. Jesus did not approach someone who needed help and say, "Are you Lutheran" or "Are you Catholic" or "Are you non-believer" before helping them. No it did not matter to him. Jesus Christ helped everyone according to their need.

April helped who needed help and it did not matter to her either what religion they belonged to. To have faith was important to her. She could only do so much. The other person (as an example the Chinese girl) April did what she felt she could do. It was encouragement and love that brought her across that finish line. Faith can move a mountain, or bring skiers through a treacherous track.

As much as April felt blown away and honored, this was too great a gift, she felt undeserving. And so during the awards ceremony, before it was over, April approached the President coming near him, as he had body guards.

He had an interpreter with him and as she neared the President she knelt before him, removed the chain from around her neck and with tears and a speech she told of why she could not accept this gift. She said she loved all people, and unluckily/ or lucky for China, she felt for this skier, and could not turn away from helping her. April said she did not deserve a key to a great city because she did the right thing.

April wanted the president to know it set a bad influence for the games. Should anyone help they should expect a great gift? No giving is from the heart and for this moment he held her heart in his hands. She felt compassion for the skier. It could have been her needing the words of encouragement. So with humility she returned the undeserved gift.

The President of the China was not angry or upset, in fact he was impressed. This small young girl was not greedy or in search of monetary things, or publicity. She was genuine, sincere and honest, a very rare trait indeed.

He felt that because of her courage, kindness and example she should have something, personal perhaps. So he lifted a finely spun gold chain from his own neck and presented it to April on a pillow. April had placed the key on the pillow and took the necklace, placing it around her neck. That gold necklace was twenty four carat gold, given to him by a close friend who valued their friendship. How befitting that this young girl also had impressed him and he valued her friendship. She knelt there for quite some time, waiting to be excused.

The President stood and walked to her, he bent over and kissed April's forehead, and said something inspiring and moving as it touched the heart of the translator and those around them.

Just to see the other cry, touched April's heart and she too had tear drops fall, it was quite an emotional and exciting moment.

As she stood up to leave there was a small procession that aligned where she was to go. Two others went with her. April was heading out of the venue to find her parents when one of the "other's ", hugged her and pointed to where her parents were.

April ran to them, she did not want to be anywhere but with them. Her Dad had out stretched arms waiting for her. It was quite a day, one that many recalled as a very heart touching moment in the Olympics. A reporter wired that story to the USA to be printed in many newspapers. Many read it, and it made them feel proud. April could have had a record time who knows? But what she did in helping the Chinese girl as far more important. To be sure, this was a feather in the cap of the USA, to win the event was exciting; to win the heart of the people was a miracle.

The next morning at the breakfast table her birth Mother read the article in the newspaper, she began to cry silently. These were tears of joy and pride. She could not have been happier to know her daughter had done so much good.

She looked around her. There was not one picture of April in their home. But she was everywhere around her and in her.

She was the beat of her heart. Nora cut out the article and placed it in her apron pocket. She would eventually put it in the scrap book that she had bought and was filling it with letters and articles about her.

On days when things did not go so well, or if arguments filled their home, she would pull out that scrap book which was a great source of comfort to her. Yes, it all seemed to work out for the good of everyone. It was not easy to let her go. Truth was she could not let her go. But she saw that God had a hand in her daughter's life, taking her places and doing things she never would have done this living with her. Yes it was hard, but she found comfort and even elation knowing her daughter was safe, excelling and setting a good example. God is good and God is great, as much as she felt God in her life she was the only one in her home.

But how wonderful it was that the little one found her way and she too had a testimony of God the father, his son Jesus Christ and the Holy Ghost. By letting go, she gave her everything.

So far as April was concerned she was done, finished! Time to go home! She made herself busy in their room packing up her clothing. In less than ten minutes she was finished. Her Mom and Dad were down stairs waiting for her.

April came out of the room, down the stairs dragging her suitcase with wheels. Stood beside her parents in the lobby, that was always busy and full with people.

"Are you ready to go?" her father asked her.

April said "yes, give me one minute ok" and she headed to the food court. The man who always watched for her was in the back cooking. She waved her arms and whistled to get his attention. He looked up and she waved, with a come here with her arms. He wiped his hands and came out. His eyes glistened it was as if he knew. April showed him her medals. He clasped his hands together, placing them to his face and bowed. April half jumped onto the counter and hugged him. The two of them did not know each other's name or background or language, but they had found a common ground, it was called friendship. When she let go she kissed him on his cheek and he stood there with tears in his eyes.

April did not understand. A woman from the back came forward she was able to speak English. She said something to them in their native language and then repeated it to April in English.

"He says he is very proud of you, he knows the struggles you had in each event. His daughter had been an Olympian and he lost her two years ago to cancer."

April's parents had joined her and stood behind her. Miranda covered her mouth with her hand as tears began. April stood there straight and strong. The woman continued. "He says that his daughter came with him to all the Olympics to meet the great winners, and she would have enjoyed meeting you."

April took his hand and said, "She already has, thru you, take heart and know your daughter is with you often. I know that you have felt her, haven't you?"

As the woman interpreted what April was saying, repeating it to the man. The man nodded as in affirmative. April said "We will all be together again, someday, and I will find you and embrace you both." Then April bowed with her hands in front of her clasped together. Then the man did the same and both of them turned to go. As they headed out to the street they planned to go to her Parents hotel where her Grandparents were. They saw many things, things April did not see with her concentration in competing. There were colors, games to play, a lot of food, people everywhere, it was a city on its own.

As they neared the hotel they noticed small golf carts with security written on the side, it was empty as if the people on it were searching for someone, or was with that someone. They went inside the hotel and headed to their room.

They preferred to take the stairs to talk.

When they entered the hallway to their room level there were security guards everywhere. Gordon was in the front and asked one of them what was wrong the guard did not answer him. Gordon felt that was rude and asked another it was a woman who said they were looking for a missing Olympian.

Gordon felt bad, and they soon entered their own room. They no more than sat down when a knock came on their door. Gordon stood up to answer it and there stood one of the guards. We are looking for April D. is she in here?

Why yes, yes she is, she is our daughter and her events are finished.

The guard was a big man but he was patient and kind. He closed the door and asked to sit down. He explained that April was an alternative to the ski jump, and she could not leave in the event they might need her for that sport.

April had forgotten all about this. She had not practiced one jump, this was nuts! The guard did not want to embarrass the family and he could see they were level headed people who did not make trouble. So he asked them to report to the outlying field house. He showed Gordon the map.

"Do you want all of us to go there?" Gordon asked,

"You all can, but it is April that must go there.

That will be her home for three more days."

Gordon took April's suitcase in hand and he was ready to go. Manny got up to join him and he reached for April's hand. April got up and went with them. The four of them headed out. The guard walked in front of them and he radioed she was found and heading to the outlying post. It was all a mistake they were getting something to eat as a family.

The guard offered the three of them a ride in the cart and they all went together. The outlying complex was at the very end of the line so to speak. At the outer edge the snow, on the very end, was the jump area.

April tugged at her father's sleeve, "Dad, I have not practiced this even once. I don't know what to do."

Her father answered her. "I am sure when you get there you will have a lot of practice jumps. Hey, they are not sure you will jump for them, it was in case they needed you right?"

Manny said, "Never be fearful, fear is of the devil, and you have no devil in you. Be brave, be strong, and fly! This is not as dangerous as Diablo, remember?"

April nodded her head yes, and added, "But I felt more comfortable with Beauty than this!"

April got out at the stop with her Dad and Grandpa and there was a coach waiting for her.

"Thought you'd skip out on us eh?

April said "No, I was with my parents."

The coach introduced himself and told April's company they were welcome to come along, but they would be out there on the jumps for about three hours. Gordon asked to use a telephone to let their wives know.

Arlan Summers had been a ski jumper himself when he was a teenager. When he married his sweetheart who was also a ski jumper, they became coaches. Charlie was a short stature, brisk walking man, with a happy, friendly way about himself.

Arlan showed the little family the ski jump which was awesome to see. It was huge, very high with a box building on top with doors that opened, for the skiers. Then there was the long ski ramp. It came down on a slope and then curled up towards the sky, for a lift for the skiers.

"Do you want to give it a try?" he asked April. "Well, is there something you should show me or tell me first, I have never jumped before" she said.

"Are you kidding me?" Arlan said. "I was under the impression that you were experienced in jumping."

"Well I am" she said, "But that would be jumping horses."

"Ok, well here we go. I will work with you today and you will have a practice jump ok?"

April was eager to learn and she did not want to make a mistake, she knew she could be hurt badly if she did not know what to do. In her mind she began to pray.

Arlan showed her how to curl down, and stretch. Then once she was out of the gate, the timer would begin. She would pick up speed fast, and when she hit the lift, it ended. She would be free in the air, falling to the ground for an extended jump. The further up and out the higher the score would be.

April practiced repeating what she saw Arlan do. "Like this" she asked, and Arlan nodded. "Let's go and try a run" Arlan said. April followed him out while Gordon and Manny stayed in the glass enclosure to watch.

Arlan and April went up to the top of the slope with a tow. There Arlan readied April for a jump. Gordon and Manny watched closely. April was in the box, goggles in place, had her ski poles with her for balance, she glanced at Arlan who gave her thumbs up.

April pushed off and went gliding down the slope. She was in a ½ crouched position and as she come to the end lift. She sprang into the air, legs apart, arms in the air, and sailed to the bottom onto the ground. She stood and looked back, there was another person who joined them, waving for April to go up the tow.

His name was Charlie he was an assistant to Arlan. So up the tow April went to the top and when she saw Arlan he told her it was ok, but she had to stay collected and off the lift. It would be better to be all together not spread out.

So down April went again, this time her form looked much better. At the top Arlan told her so and he said a few more jumps and then they would call it the end. April came down the slope and her distance was about thirty yards.

Arlan and Charlie consulted one another and they thought that April had a good chance to medal because of her slight frame and the way she could get a lift and air travel down the slope for distance. That is if she was needed. When finished April rejoined her Grandfather who was very supportive while Arlan and Charlie spoke with Gordon, he said if she would stay collected she would have a much better chance.

They all headed back to "home" Gordon was anxious to speak to Miranda, and tell her all about the ski jump lessons and how April did. April of course did not go with them she had to stay in the hotel with the other skiers American skiers.

April knocked at a door with the number 2 on it an older woman answered the door, "Hi my name is April, I was told to come and stay in this dorm."

The woman smiled and said, "Welcome, come on in"

As April entered the room there was only one other woman there. April waved Hi to her and just stood there.

The other woman had dark black hair that made her beautiful skin striking the other woman had brunette hair and was tall. April looked at the woman and asked, "Is there a bed for me?" She said, "Of course, forgive me I am a bit tired, here let me help you,"

She took April's bag and put it on the window sill, the bed was right in front of that. She sat on the bed and excitedly asked her what sport April was in.

April looked at her and said, "I am an alternate for the ski jump, I had several practice jumps today."

The woman grabbed both of April's shoulders and excitedly said, "You go girl and nail that landing" By now the other woman came over and the two of them questioned April. "You watch sometimes they like to screw with your minds, if you don't feel like jumping at that particular time, tell them you have to go to the bathroom. Tell them you must go, you know #2, or that you are sick and need to vomit. That will delay them and they will put another jumper there. I have done that and it quiets my nerves. That went on for about ten minutes when April began to yawn.

"Oh my gosh it's almost 9:00, you had better get to bed" the one said.

"I know, but I'd like to take a shower first, if that's alright."

"Of course it is, you go on and we will be going to bed too, we are not sure if we are running tomorrow, but we have to be there early in case we are called."

"What do you both do?" April asked.

"Who us? We are downhill slalom racers, and we are dying to get out there, do our run and have this over with." They said.

With that April got up to shower, and that hot water was wonderful. It was so good to have the hot water hit her muscles and relax. She was done in no time and dried herself and slipped on her PJ,'s. She came out and both the girls were in bed, one was wearing an eye mask. They had twin beds that were just a few feet apart April's bed was at the other wall by the window. She slipped into her bed and was out, fast asleep in no time.

As usual April was up early 4 a.m. She was very quiet and did not wake the other two women. She took her clothes and dressed in the bathroom. Then she gathered what she needed and slipped out of the room without waking the girls.

She headed to the closest food court and there she had a quick breakfast of rice cereal and milk with a banana. Then she headed out to the ski slopes.

At the slopes there were people out there working already. April sat in the lounge area and watched them she even dozed off for a bit. April knew that they would be competing in the morning early. That is what the coach said to her.

Sure enough along came Arlan and he had paperwork with him. He saw April and waved to her, he came into the lounge area and sat down beside her. "You need to sign this paper that shows you are a part of the jumping team."

There are two other girls jumping for the U.S." April took his pen and wrote down her name. "Ok, let's get going" he said. "I don't' know where Katlin or Breanna are, but they knew to be out here early." He and April rode the tow up the hill.

"What order are we in" April asked him. "I don't know, sometimes we are first and sometimes we are last. No matter if you jump well or bad, you will always have the option of a 2nd jump, so don't worry." They were at the top and there were several other girls there from other countries. April knew not to talk to them but to let things be. Soon April saw two other girls dressed in the same color ski clothes as she had and guessed they were Katlin and Breanna.

April walked over to them and said "Hey, I'm April and I guess I am jumping with you for the U.S." "Yeah I heard about you, and personally I think it sucks, we have spent years practicing, have been hurt and injured in this sport. You come along as "all hail April". You don't' know anything about jumping." It was obvious she was angry April was there.

The other girl Breanna said nothing, either she did not agree with her partner or she did not want to anger her or April. April appreciated that. "if you can't say anything nice, then don't say anything at all" is the motto her Mother taught her. It is not fun to participate as a member of a team and be treated so ignorantly. April did not ask to be there, she was ready to go home they looked for her and brought her here.

April tapped Katlin on her back to turn around and said "Look, I did not want to be here, I was on my way home when the security guards came looking for me. They found me and brought me here. So keep your negative comments to yourself.

We are a team, so how about acting like it" Katlin was shocked she was the natural leader in the ski jumping and this up start startled her, and then she laughed. "Let's see how good you do out there" and she pointed to the slope. "Well Katlin I hope we all do well, for our country" April replied. As she sat there with the others, soon Breanna came and sat by her.

Breanne said. "Don't mind Katlin she is just bossy, it's her nature. I let her go and don't say much, she is all mouth, believe me." And with that, Katlin was called for her first jump.

"Rip it Kate" Breanne called to her. Katlin waved to her teammate, "Do your best Kate" April shouted to her. Katlin gave April a thumb up. Soon all the girls were lined up. April was to jump before Breanne and soon she was standing on the platform, feeling a buzz and then off she went.

She crouched down low and went whizzing down the slope and as she neared the end she jumped up, kept her legs together as best as she could, her skis tipped up to the wind and she floated down, down, down. She made a decent jump putting her in the fifth position on the leader board. That angered some other girls they rudely passed her knocking into her shoulders.

She saw her 2nd coach Charlie he came to her and said "You did really well for your first jump, now you have one more after everyone is done on round one.

April asked Charlie how she could improve, "Well, it's hard to say sometimes people get a lift of wind to help them, but it's all in the part of the game."

April saw the girls Katlin and Breanne, and Breanne said she was 2nd on the leader board, Katelin was in 8th position.

"So don't brag" she said to April. "I'm not" April said, "I was kidding you. You know that I don't know much about this sport, I am here to help in any way I can." "Don't be so humble" Katlin said, "You're jump was pretty awesome." So the three of them had a group hug and headed back up for their 2nd jump.

Breanne would go last because she was a serious contender on the leader board. As the girls make their jump, April bowed her head and said a prayer silently. She stayed in that still position for about two minutes. Then she heard her name called. She really was not ready, but hey, why not! She was prepared she knew what to do, so go for it!

April stepped up, adjusted her gloves and goggles, turned her head one way or another to loosen the muscles and turned to the man at the gate and nodded, she was ready. She heard the beep of the timer and on beep five the gate would open and that would be her last run.

April shoved off and crouched down, she knew she was picking up speed and was going faster than her first run. She felt the wind at her back and she worried it would blow her off course. As April come down the ramp, she felt worried but then thought why? Why am I afraid?

That is crazy I am here to help and this is my best shot. As she lifted up off of the ramp the wind boosted her higher. She kept her legs straight and skis in front of her face her poles were at her side, she was completely free! She was flying, literally.

The crowed was afraid she would land on top of them and backed up out of the way. April was beginning to come down and still traveled a little further. April landed near the line of where the spectators were. The announcer said that April D. was now in

The Girl in the Mirror Book 3

second place. April was speechless! She never thought she would do well. She managed to battle the wind and land, and she was grateful for that. She never thought she would take second place. Now there were eight more skiers to come down and take over, she watched closely.

Breanne beat her distance. Breanne and Katlin both hit April on the back to congratulate her. April told them how she felt and they laughed. Sometimes when a beginner is in competition or a card game or most anything, they do well. It's crazy but true.

As it turned out April got the silver medal and Breanne got the gold medal. She and April held hands at the Medals ceremony. April was happy it was so unexpected. There is no way that the Olympics can say she did not do her share in helping.

April's parents and grandparents were there as usual Mom and Contessa both were crying Dad and Manny were beaming. And there was another woman with them. She was short in stature with dark black hair, small features. She looked Native American to April. April wondered who she was.

The award ceremony happened without incident. April was relieved to be with her parents. She was done, no more and now she wanted to stay for the closing ceremony. Say goodbye to her friends and then go. Oh how she longed to go home!

As they walked out of the Olympic awards building Miranda put April next to the woman and said "I think you two should talk." Miranda and the three others continued on while April and the woman stood there. The woman said, "Would you like to sit down somewhere?" They found a picnic bench setting and sat down. The woman asked April, "Do you know who I am? Can you guess?" April looked at the woman and then noticed her eyes. They were like hers. Her nose was like April's too, short and pudgy. As April studied the woman's face tears began to slowly trickle from her eyes. The woman touched April's arm and asked, "Do you remember me at all" April felt she knew her voice, she closed her eyes trying to remember, but she could not bring any memories forth and told the woman.

April stood up to embrace her and the two of them held onto each other for a long, long time.

"What is your name?" April asked her.

"Nora, my name is Nora" the woman said.

April sat by the woman and told her "Our eyes are the same, so are our noses and are your ears crinkled too?" The woman showed April her ears, and indeed hers were just like April's.

"I am so glad to meet you. I have been so busy training for the Olympics. I hope you got to see some of them" April said to her. "I did, you see I got a call from your Mother, (she said that so easily) who offered me a ride to the Olympics to watch you and I was thrilled! Your parents did not let me pay for anything. She said.

April replied, "Yes that is how they are and they taught me to be the same way, would you like to get something to eat or drink" April asked Nora.

"Yes, something to drink maybe" Nora said.

They went to the Olympic cafeteria and sat down, April asked the woman what she would like, "Oh a coffee for me" she said. "Coffee? April asked the woman "Are you sure? It's not good for you, you know."

"Why is it not good for me?" the woman asked her.

"It can give you higher blood pressure or ulcers."

It can make you addicted to the caffeine."

The woman asked April to get her what she thought would be good. April came back with two large hot chocolates with marshmellows, "Here you go, one for you and one for me." Nora said, "You loved hot chocolate as a little girl, you often would come to me with a cup and say, "Chawlit" and Nora smiled.

Then the conversation turned to what Nora often thought about. Nora told her "You were the light and delight of my life. You see I had nine boys, and you were the only girl." "I had many things planned for you, to teach you how to cook, and bake, how to can goods for winter. And I wanted to comb your hair and see you to the prom and on your wedding day" and she began to cry.

April put her arm around her and said, "Please don't cry, you will still get to do many of those things. I would be honored if you helped me on my prom day and if you would be in my wedding someday. I know my Mom, and April stopped. The woman patted her hand saying, "It's alright"

April continued, "She would like that too, she is very kind and a peaceful woman." "Where are you staying?" April asked her. "In a hotel room near your parents" I have never been taken such good care of in my life" Nora said.

"They have been so good to me, and to you too, I see." April nodded her head yes. "I hope this is not hard for you, I was a bit nervous to come, but I felt it was time and I was so impressed with your bravery in these events. You have been taught well that was evident in your ski race, helping the Chinese girl."

"I look at you and I now I am glad, so very glad you are where you are. I will always and forever love you. But I could never have given you wings to fly. I never could have provided for you as your parents have. You have two good parents, if you had stayed with me there would only have been one. It would have been very hard on me to do anything without his approval.

April understood, she herself felt that one day when she did marry it would have to be with someone who was like her. Who liked some of that she did such as riding, or athletic things. She never wanted to be bound to someone who did nothing or someone with a bad temper or attitude. Nope she hoped for a happy, caring person, someone who was slow to anger.

The two of them sat there for over two hours talking and laughing, asking questions, and then they looked at their watches and knew it was time to go. So they walked together to the Di Angelo's and Fortinado's hotel room. April knocked at the door and Gordon welcomed both of them in. April was tired. She left to sleep and left Nora with her family.

The next day her friends Peter and Hal were speed skating. April was determined to go, so she and her family bought tickets and they there from the start to finish. They sat with Jinks and his wife, and they were so surprised and happy.

April sat by Miranka, they hugged at meeting. April's family blended with Jinks and his wife. It was a great time together. Her birth Mother left to go home. April was glad, not that she was gone, but there was a lot for Nora to think about.

As the speed skating began like a switch the Hal and Peter's family tuned in. They breathed it in. It was intense with much hollering and loud yelling at the skaters. April was so glad her parents did not do that to her, she did her thing.

Hal and Peter were fast, they really excelled, "poured it on" as Hal would say. They took first in all of their events, Poland was extremely proud of them, they loved these boys immensely. They threw flowers and cheered at them. They responded with smiles, waving at them, throwing kisses with their hands.

It was all over far too soon. Both families loved watching the racing, the time, the pacing for energy, passing one another. It was amazing and so intricately done. And then it was over. Then the end of games ceremony would begin. April went in with many other competitors and traded for small trinkets.

There were pins and many autographs. They all participated Many had parts to play. Some sang along. Some danced and it was all in fun and April had the time of her life, she never laughed harder.

All too soon they were packing their bags and heading for the airport to go home. April had Mirinka's address in her bags and Promised to stay in touch with her. To have a friend, you must be a friend.

At the airport, there were many who waved at April and her family, some took pictures and others spoke to them, shaking their hands. Contessa said she never felt so important in her life, and her husband Manny squeezed her to him and said "That is not true and you know it." She looked at him and said "Yes, you are right, you have always treated me like a queen, forgive me sweetheart." and he kissed her cheek.

Their bags were minimal but still they had to check them in and the handlers helped them. They approached the ticket terminal and showed their return tickets. Everything was in order but April had to travel in 3rd class, because the Olympics never overspend unnecessarily. That did not sit well with Miranda. She insisted April sit with them.

"I have been away from my daughter for months! Do you understand how I feel?" she said to the woman at the counter. "I do not care if I have to pay more money, I insist, I want my daughter with me and she began to cry." The manager saw this and quickly came over. His English was broken and he tried to console her. When he realized what Miranda was talking about, that her daughter was a competitor in the Olympics and had won three medals. He did not question the woman any longer he made sure April's seat was up graded to first class and made sure she sat with her family, as a family.

As they began to board, many of the people waved to April, some grabbed her hand to shake it. Some young children wanted her autograph pulling out paper or a photo of April taken at the Olympics. Photos April had not seen. She looked up at her Mom who said, "I have them all" and April laughed. April should have known better.

Once on the airplane everyone settled down, some looked at April and bowed their head as in "Hi" and April would wave at them. She was taught to be polite it never was good to be rude.

The flight was awesome, it was the only real sleep April had in months. With ear plugs she would sleep, wake up for two minutes and go back to sleep. Her parents realized the work she had to do to get ready.

The grueling workouts that she made look easy. Her father beamed at his daughter. He took her small hand in his and looked at how small her hand really was. He also realized the strength she had within her.

April either read or made up a quote and would say it often, "If your mind can perceive it, your heart will receive it and your hands can achieve it" Gordon found that quote to be profound. That was the way his daughter lived, she believed anything she tried she would give 100%. To do less was an insult to her.

But holding her hand, so small, he was amazed, they have been a family for seven years. He reminisced at the many things they had done together, one of the most important was April was the binding that brought Miranda's parents close to them all. Finally, Manny and Contessa treated him as a son and they doted on April. And she loved them right back it was nothing for April to kiss her Grandmothers hand as they were walking. Contessa would dismiss it as if it was foolish, when Gordon saw Contessa put the back of her hand April had kissed against her cheek.

Yes, this little girl not so long ago surely changed their lives. Here they were flying on an airplane heading back to the U.S. when the only time Gordon flew was when he was in the military. Words could never express the love he had for her

No matter that people would say, that they did not have the same blood. Their hearts matched they were and would forever be family. She was their Daughter! He looked at his wife who was asleep with her head against the back rest and April's head on her shoulder

They flew to Germany and had an exchange of airplanes to board for America. While they were in Germany they did some shopping. The women looked for household things, new interesting things or a memory of this trip. April found a red horse that was about six inches high with shiny black hooves. It reminded her of Native Son, and she wanted it. The cost was eight American dollars, which she had no money. She went to her Dad to ask him but Manny beat him. He pulled out a wad of money and put it in her hand. "Here, you go shopping" he said. April was aghast she never spent money like that. "No, no I can't take this, I only need eight dollars Grandpa" she said. Grandpa said, "Humph, you are wise but also a cheap date" and he laughed at her".

April was thrilled with her little trinket, she planned to one day have a truck and place this on the dashboard, that way he would always be with her. April thought about him all the time. When she least expected, his nicker or his body would pop in her head. The races they had or the rides on the open fields

Crossing that finish line with no one near them, yes, she missed him immensely. He had made an imprint on her heart, and to say she loved him was an understatement.

They arrived in the U.S. in New York, there was such a swarm of people as they came down the tarmac, and then the singing began. They were singing the song America. When they saw April they began to cheer and shout to her. It was so surreal, and unexpected. Security began to escort April as the throngs of people began to surge towards her. April was unaware of the possible danger that existed. So her parents were grateful that security acted on April's behalf.

April waved to them and signed some autographs, she talked to many of them and laughed a lot, Gordon was amazed at how social she was with total strangers. In that way, she and Gordon were nothing alike. Her Mother was not open to people either. Where ever she got that talent from he did not know.

But there she was chatting and touching their shoulders and laughing with them. Thankfully the security kept April moving along, to reach the inside of the terminal and to their next airplane.

They would fly from New York to California straight no stops, no layovers. They were escorted into a room in the airport. The security asked them to stay there to be safe

If they needed or wanted anything they would get it for them. Miranda knew the next leg of their flight would be a long one and suggested that they eat a meal, and stretch their legs.

So a security guard escorted them past offices, down long corridors and long halls to a gym, and there they met a young woman who would get whatever they wanted for a meal in the terminal for them.

"What do you like to eat as a meal? She asked them.

"What do you suggest" Miranda asked the young woman.

"Well when I have time to eat decent I go to the corner place where Miguel makes the best homemade dinners. He has meatloaf, lasagna, and many other things, let me run and get you a menu since you have an hours lay over."

She must have run fast because she was back in a matter of minutes. Miranda and Contessa browsed through the menu it made no sense for either Manny or Gordon to look because each of them ate what their wives ate.

It was always like that and April could not get over it. She said she was an individual and liked other things, but in the end she admitted what they had was just fine with her too.

In less than fifteen minutes a lovely dinner was on their tables, in Styrofoam boxes.

Gordon and Miranda had the Meatloaf dinners. Manny and Contessa had the Lasagna dinners. April had the chicken salad with broccoli cheese soup.

They did not get a bill and Gordon stood up and went out

to the girl concerned to ask her about it. "No sir, the owner will be paid by the Airport, you see your daughter is a celebrity here in the U. S. you may not understand this or comprehend fully what your daughter has done for pride, and making happiness here in the states. Everyone was rooting for her, this young girl attempting such big things and she would win. That ski race was something else, wasn't it?" "Um, um, that girl has heart to get that Chinese girl up to cross that finish line. Why someone else would never have tried, they would have left that Chinese girl behind crossing that finish line. But not her, that's what makes her a winner she has heart and soul of gold."

"So for that reason, here with us, sky is the limit, we are honored to have you here with us. This to us is a one in a million chance, when will someone do as she has come through our terminal?"

"Please let us do this small thing for your family and famous daughter" she said. Gordon was a little taken aback, his daughter never would see herself as a hero, or worthy of free anything.

Because they raised her to understand that nothing is free, someone worked for it. Gordon thanked her and asked her to be sure to let her boss know of their gratitude, and mentally he would remember to fly this airline if they could when they needed to fly.

Gordon came back and everyone complained they were stuffed, except April. She was eating a piece of coconut cream pie. "How did they know this was my favorite?" she asked.

Gordon shrugged his shoulders to her but inside he knew, he knew that the world who was interested would know anything and everything about her. The size of her clothing, what she liked to eat, the music she listened to, what she did for hobbies, on and on. That is how it is with anyone who reaches fame status. Hopefully at home, folks will understand April better and treat her as they always had, hopefully.

They all washed with the towelettes that were provided to them. A short while later a knock came on their door. They were to be boarding on their next flight, a direct flight to California. They all got up and followed the girl. April reached to squeeze her hand and thanked her.

As they reached the last door the girl stopped and peeked out the small crack of the door.

The security guards were coming in all ten of them, in front of her family, behind them and on both sides. On each side of April they blocked her so she was not so easy to see.

There was no incident to their terminal and boarding their last flight home. They all sat in their seats, sitting with each other. Most of the passengers did not notice her, only a few did, they smiled and waved. One reached over to thank her and shake her hand. When the pilot came on line to make his announcements, he spilled the beans.

He said there was a now famous athlete on their plane. He told them who she was and what accomplishments she had made. He asked them to give her a round of applause, which made April turn red as a strawberry.

"Mom" she said as she pulled on her Mothers sleeve, "Why did he say all of that?" "Well, probably because he followed what you did, the stories were on TV every night and in the newspapers, he must feel proud of you. That's all, its normal." Just don't let this get to your head, stay calm and cool as a cucumber.

Miranda squeezed her daughter to her, a hug that lasted a good ten seconds.

The Di Angelo Family and company flew home to California. It was a long flight that they chatted, played hang man's bluff, tic tac-toe and read books. April even wrote a letter to her friend Marinka to be ready to send to her when she arrived home. Home what a lovely sound that had.

They landed in Los Angeles. They had a fast run to the gate on a commuter with Scott flew to Fresno. Once inside they were quiet anticipating being home. They saw the landscapes and could point out many of the homes and land that they saw. The pilot Scott knew April very well, but again due to the Olympics and her picture in the papers. He buzzed over the area where Native Son was housed and April swore she saw him outside at a feeder which excited her more than the three medals she had earned.

The pilot brought the plane in for a landing it was smooth and even. When Scott took April's hand he was grinning and said, "We are so proud of you, for the spirit of sisterhood you brought to the games. We promise to let you be you. You certainly deserve it"

Parade and Picnic

And that was that. No one made a big fuss, one parade down Main Street and a barbeque in the park that was it. April was happy to accommodate them it gave her an opportunity to see all those she loved and lived around.

The people of Fresno all chipped in and made something to take to the parade, blowers, confetti, candy and all sort of things.

They sat on rugs, their coats and on chairs. Some sat on their porches and the balcony's. There were kids on light poles, just to see the Sheriff, now that was more their liking. The parade was alright, April waved and smiled but she felt a bit silly.

She threw candy, but what else could she could do?

The picnic on the other hand was awesome! There were all sorts of food to eat and people would come up to her, introduce themselves. They told her where they lived, or April would ask and she hugged every one of them.

One young woman with two very small children was overheard talking to her husband, she said "What a nice young girl, I mean they are not rich, she works hard, and just won three medals for the USA and she is as sweet and humble as you get. I am impressed!"

April sat with some friends with a plate of sweetcorn and a hamburger. She missed fresh food having been in the winter of Poland. The food tasted heavenly, she just wanted to take a bite and hold it in her mouth and really savor it. Her friends made fun of her, but she didn't care. Many of them asked what the Olympics were like, and April told them honestly.

From training to competition, some were spell bound, "The worse thing was being away from my family and YOU" and they laughed. It was awesome to be home. Home where she could truly be herself, no one judged her, not that she knew about anyway.

The Marshalls came and Hugh found her and he picked her up and hugged her, so did Trevor. "Man that was awesome we got to stay up late to watch the Olympics when you were on." Trevor said.

Mrs. Marshall hugged April and told her they were all so proud of her, that what she did was not an easy thing, although knowing April she would make it simple, but she wanted to thank her. So did Mr. Marshall. He said, "You gave America another reason to be proud." April smiled, and well, she was a bit embarrassed. If everyone did the right thing this world would be even more of a wonderful place to live in. But she got it, and understood.

Hugh and April sat on chairs by the fire, they spoke little but he kept looking at her curiously. "Do you want S'mores or some soda" he asked her.

"No, I am fine, just sitting here with you" she said, and she truly was content.

After it got dark someone came with a guitar and began to play. He was very talented. Soon along came Mr. O'Toole and he had bagpipes with him. He was smiling from ear to ear. "Oh Boy," Hugh said elbowing April in her side. April got up and graciously took the bagpipes and kissed Mr. O'Toole on his cheek. She put the pipes on and gave them a try as it had been a while.

Soon she was playing a lovely ballad it was a Scottish tune full of delightful and sad notes. April knew the notes by heart, she did not notice some women with tears, or how some turned away but stayed in the same spot. Her Mom and Dad heard the bagpipes as did the Marshalls and they came to the fire to listen. Gordon put her arms around his wife as they both stood watching their daughter play. "It's so beautiful" Miranda said, "Yes, it is, and so is she" and Gordon noticed Hugh watching his daughter intently. And Trevor was off chasing some other girls. He like Hugh a lot but April was far too young to be serious with anyone he would have to watch out for them.

The bagpipe song ended and many clapped. Then she played a lively tune everyone clapped to the beat. April took the pipes off and handed them to her Mother. Mom put them on backwards to be able to carry them around with her until she found Mr. O'Toole to put them in the proper case. It was late after 10:00 p. m. and April was exhausted.

It had been a lot to do since they arrived home. She fell into the routine again of home. But there was the parade and many telephone calls and interviews. April just wanted to relax, that is why she looked forward to the barbeque.

April sat down again and yawned,

"Are you tired April?" Hugh asked her.

"I am but I don't want to go home yet" she said.

"I don't want you to go yet either" he said to her.

He leaned forward and kissed her smack on her lips.

April froze, she liked Hugh. She loved his friendship. But she felt afraid.

So she quickly, silently, she said a prayer and along came her Mom, and sat down beside April.

"So, are you ready to go home April dear?" I just said to Hugh that I was tired but I really did not want to go home yet." "But since you are here, I don't have to go and find you." April smiled at her Mother.

"Well to be truthful I am very tired, it has been many long days." Miranda said.

Hugh spoke up quickly and said, "If April wants to stay, I'd gladly take her home when she is ready."

Gordon just happened to be standing a few feet away from where Miranda sat and he piped up.

"That ok Hugh, we have not had April home very long and we really like having her with us." "I am sure you understand." "Oh, yes Sir, I do I was just offering", Hugh said.

"You are such an agreeable fellow Hugh."

"We might take you up on that offer another time, but for now all of the Di Angelos are tired and it is time to go home and hit the sack so to speak" Gordon said.

April got up and touched Hugh on his shoulder and thanked him and said she'd see him again soon. April's parents were already walking out and she quickly followed them.

The Dilemma

Back in Pennsylvania, Nora was picked up at the airport by her father in law. He had many questions for her. They pulled over at a small café and she told him all she knew. He was a silent and strong man. Although he never said it, he loved that little girl and hurt just as much as the mother when she disappeared. He and April were like kindred souls, with much in common. Often he thought about her and now the reality sunk in. He was elated that she did so well in the Olympics. She was brave, strong. He laughed out loud. He was very proud of her.

"Did they say if anyone could come out and see her" he asked Nora.

"No they did not say that, but I am sure if you asked and explained who you were, they would be glad to have you." "These people are extremely kind and generous." "April is the same way, a gentle young woman with kindness in her touch." And the Grandfather smiled. "You must keep this a secret" he said to Nora."

"She" would not like that I would go, especially to see her, and he shook his head. He would never comprehend the hate his wife had for the little girl. She always had it out for her, pinching her to make her cry, telling her she was bad girl.

Often he took April outside, put her on a swing and push her so high into the top three branches, up high. She never screamed. She laughed with delight she said it tickled her belly inside. He tried his best to keep "her" away from April, to keep April safe.

Yes, he ached for this little one, and now she had been found. She is happy, well adjusted, achieving, and growing and he wanted to be a part of her life. Every now and then and he wanted Nora to make the arrangements soon.

Nora slipped several photos of April that were taken at the Olympics on to the seat and told him to put them in his pocket. The pictures were one with her flying high in her last jump and one with her ski racing, encouraging the Chinese girl to get up.

She was wearing a silly hat that everyone identified and knew who was wearing it. Another photo with April on the medals stand, she was kissing all of her medals. He did not know what was in the photos until later. That simple act of kindness sealed a bond between him and his daughter-in-law. She did not have to give them to him. He kept them hidden and would study her face late at night. It surely was her and she had his blood within her veins.

Nora encouraged him to write to the family and let them know that within a month he would like to come for a visit he would take lodging in a hotel that was close, if that was possible.

He always had a close relationship with April and protected her as much as he could.

Grandpa was ashamed of how his son treated April. He had to reassure them, his heart was broke no it was shattered when April disappeared. He made it clear they could not call him and explained why. It was his trip to California, and was a pretense of going to Portugal. The letter was mailed out the next day.

Back in Fresno, that night April knew her parents were tired, it showed. She desperately wanted to talk to her Mom about

Hugh. April did not know what to do or how to handle herself. She liked Hugh tons.

But she did not feel comfortable with him kissing her, especially in front of other people.

So she kept quiet about it to wait for an opportunity the next day. Surely there would be a quiet moment with her Mom. So they all showered and headed to bed. Her bed her pillow and Ruby, there was nothing better. These three simple things she missed most at night. Right now, she did not think one more thing, she was lost, asleep, she was content and exhausted.

The next day after chores were done, the ponies fed, the chicken fed, eggs gathered & setting on the porch. The calves all fed, and she took Ruby with her on the 4 wheeler. She had found a pair of dog goggles in Poland. They were so cool, and this way Ruby could see and her eyes would not water. Ruby loved it. She became the side companion on every 4 wheel ride.

That afternoon when Dad was at work and dinner was laid out for evening cooking April's Mom was in the living room reading the newspaper and April came up to her.

"Mom, can I talk to you?" she asked.

Without looking up Miranda said "What? What do you want to talk about?" and she kept reading the paper.

"Mom I need you, I really need to talk to you." April urged. Miranda turned down the corner of the newspaper and asked her again, "What do you want to talk about?"

April felt embarrassed, stupid and almost began to cry. Miranda saw this and put the newspaper aside and stood up. She took April by the hand taking her to the couch and they both sat down.

Miranda sort of flopped April's bottom and said, "Come on now girl, tell your Mom, what is it?" April leaned her head on her Mom and Miranda felt her chest becoming wet. Miranda stroked her daughters head and hair, cooing to her. "Come on, I am here, you can tell me. You can talk to me about anything." "Are you lonely?"

"Are you missing Poland and your friends there?" Each time April shook her head no. "Are you having trouble here with something or someone?" April was still, and Miranda said "I know it is not me or Dad, is it?" She felt April's head shake no. "Someone else, hum…. Is it a boy or a girl?" April stayed still. "Hum, so I have to guess, I know that you like all your girlfriends and you don't have many if any quarrels with them, so it has to be a boy, is it Hugh?" and April began to cry.

Miranda pulled April up to her so she could look into her face. "Did he say anything to you honey?"

"No he kissed me and I was not ready, I mean, I was not expecting it and well….

I like Hugh an awful lot but I am not ready to be his girl, his date, his one and only. Miranda had a smile on her face but she knew she dared not to laugh, it would crush April.

"Well I understand how you feel, and you are entitled to your feelings. Hugh is nineteen and you are fifteen that is a difference and in hormones, a HUGE difference." "You do not need to offer him anything, just be yourself and tell him how you feel. If you are uncomfortable, tell him, be honest." "But I don't want to lose him as a friend" April said. Miranda answered her, "A good friend would understand. A good friend would never make his friend feel uncomfortable. If they liked you that much they would not

pressure you or make you feel like you had to make a choice."
"Don't take this so seriously, stand your ground. Make it clear to
him and keep the lines of communication open". April kissed her
Mother and said, "Thanks Mom, You're so smart". Miranda said,
"For now, there will come a time when you will not think so,
watch and see." and she kissed her daughters head.

"Now you go and wash up ok, Dad will be home a little early
and I need to get dinner together" Miranda said. April headed up
stairs and Miranda headed to the kitchen and picked up the phone
and called her best friend and companion.

She spoke with him about April keeping it light. Gordon said
he needed to think about it for a while and will speak to Miranda
tonight when they retired for bed.

Soon the chicken parmesan was in the oven, spaghetti boiling
in the pot of water, Garlic bread ready to be popped in the oven
for ten minutes before they sit down for dinner at five.

Lois

The real help since April was back was the milking. It was all done by sweet Beth, who was taking some time off. Beth wanted to bring her Mom Lois to be near. Beth's Mother Lois was ill and the family wanted Beth to bring her to the farm and spend time with Mrs. Adams. They two of them chatted almost all day long.

Di Angelo's made sure there was a Nurse that came weekly to check vital signs and see that all her medical needs were met. When Beth heard the Di Angelo's plans, she cried. She loved her Mom so much and wanted to spend time with her. How perfect! She could still work, make a good living, no expenses to her and time with her Mom. Lois flourished on the farm. Beth and Lois went for daily walks in the yard. Lois gardened a bit, planting flowers and vegetables. It was wonderful to see the two of them together and how kind it was of them to include Mrs. Adams. The three of them were so very happy.

Beth's had said she believed it was the happiest she had seen her Mom in years.

Beth's Mother Lois encouraged Beth to get her education. It was difficult because Beth's father had passed away the year Beth graduated from High School. Lois kept working as a secretary in the school, so Beth could get her education in Nursing. No Mother was prouder at Beth's graduation with honors. How wonderful that now out of need, they all could spend quality time together.

They had time to talk, eat, shop, laugh, cry, pray and reminisce. Out of need, everything came together. The Doctor in Fresno was amazed at how fast Lois responded to the quality of farm life. She bubbled with stories of the flowers budding.

Lois even brought the office some of them. Lois was happy and her COPD was actually improving. Yes, she became out of breath with a fast pace, but there was no fast pace here. Lois could do what she wanted when she wanted. She had no responsibilities, no stress. Lois could nap or go out for ice tea in the yard with a friend. Lois had always wanted a cat and now she had one that was Mrs. Adams and Scooter the cat loved Beth's Mom. He would curl up on her lap in the yard or at her feet as she slept in bed. No bills to pay, nothing to buy unless she wanted it meaning small soap or personal things.

If it were anything else, the Di Angelo's stepped in and helped her. Lois did not have to pay for any medications or if it were medical needs that was all taken care of. Beth felt a little overwhelmed at the generosity and spoke to Gordon about this. He told her, she alleviated a HUGE burden to their family milking for them. Beth said she enjoyed milking she paid attention but also had time to think and reflect.

To let you all know Beth's Mother Lois lived with Beth and Mrs. Adams for eight years, which Beth said they were the best years of her life. Lois took a painting class at the senior center and was very good. She and Mr. Jones had become good friends there and arch enemies in painting class.

Each of them was wanting to do better than the other. Beth had never seen her Mother laugh so much, or so at peace with life.

So Back To The Dilemma:

What April felt with Hugh was quite simple to Gordon, Stop seeing him! April was aghast she did not want to do that. So the next step was to have April tell Hugh the truth. So April did what she had been counseled to do, over and over. She picked up the phone to call Jude Du Val to see if she could see him today. As it was, he was out for the minute, but Missy said to come right down, the Judge was would be right back.

April got her bike out and put the kick stand up she hollered to her Mother that she was leaving for a ride. She did not tell her where or to see whom. April pedaled her bike the distance to town. On Main Street the headed to the city hall, she parked her bicycle, put the chain on and walked inside. She knew to walk to the back side to the Judge's chambers and knock. Missy answered the door and let her in, hugging her as she entered.

"He just got back, was freshening up in the bathroom" she said. Judge Du Val came out and gave April a high five. "What brings you out here toots" he said. "Well, you said if I ever had a problem or needed help to talk to you, and now I need you to talk to" she said. The Judge came out and sat down on his chair. He leaned back with his feet on the desk, (no shoes) and said

"Hit me." April pulled up a chair and sat down. Her head was down and she said, "I don't know where to start."

"Come on, head up" he said "talk to me."

"Well, it's about a boy. He kissed me. I was not ready and it frightened me." "You see, he is a good friend, my best friend. I don't want to lose his friendship. We do a lot of things together" April said.

"Well, I can see your concern" he said. "May I ask who this person is?"

"Well, it's Hugh. I know you know him. He is so nice she said. "Yes, he is and he is a great catch" the Judge said.

"But I was not fishing for a catch. I like my life like it is. I am not his age, and everyone thinks I am mature but I am not as mature as he is. Hugh is nineteen."

"Oh yes, yes, I see" The Judge said, "How about I speak with Hugh, as a friend. You see I am not your parent or a sheriff" and he winked at her. "So let me speak to Hugh. He has a level head and I believe this is a misunderstanding."

April looked at him with hope and breathed a sigh of relief. "I am thankful and so glad you can help me" she said. "Hey I told you, ANYTIME!" he said to her. April hugged him and left. She was still shaking but feeling some relief and pedaled home. The Judge had his 2:00 hearing and then changed into street duds.

He said Good Night to Missy and left. He drove through town to the countryside, up to the hills and green pine trees to the Marshalls home.

He was in luck, Hugh was home. He saw Hugh and Trevor having a water battle in their back yard as he pulled into their driveway. The Judge knocked on their door and Mrs. Marshall answered. "Oh hello" she said, "What brings you out to our neck of the woods." "Well, not much, I just wanted to talk with Hugh.

I know he is graduating this year and I wanted to talk to him about career options" he said.

"Oh how I wish you would" she confided in him, "You see, Hugh wants to enter the military, and make a career out of it."

"Oh wow, well that certainly is honorable, maybe his mind is made up" Du Val said.

"Yes, it is, but maybe, just maybe if you speak to him he might want to change his mind or mull it over. Mrs. Marshall said So she called Hugh up to the deck, "Hugh I believe you know Mr. Du Val", she said. The Judge reached out and shook Hugh's hand. "Hugh I was hoping you'd go with me for a bit, maybe a ride to the hills, and we can talk." Hugh threw on shorts and a shirt and they left. Hugh hoped into the passenger side of the Judge's truck. They left and headed for high country a half hour ride.

When Hugh spoke up and said, "For a Judge you could use an upgrade" and he laughed at the Judge.

They drove up to a high area and could see much of the valley below, it was beautiful. They saw an Eagle that flew past them. She obviously had a nest on the side ridge.

Hugh was sure the Judge was there to talk him out of entering the military but he already had made up his mind. He was graduating in June, and was ready.

Imagine his shock when the conversation turned to April. "Well Hugh I chose to speak to you rather than her father." "You know with him being the Sheriff and all."

"You see Hugh there is an age difference between the two of you." "I believe I know where you are, I was once nineteen too." "Believe me April is not where you are emotionally." "She is innocent and still very young you know."

"You know she races horses. She Volunteers everywhere and

anywhere. She had a lot of work to do at home. Frankly she thinks you are her absolute best friend. I believe if asked she would lay down her life for you. But she is not ready for a relationship of a steady boyfriend and all that comes with it. April has no time. You know yourself that on Mutual days she is there for two hours best and then home.

April is always in bed by 9 or 9:30 absolutely no later, because she is up at 4:00 a.m."

"So can you understand her?" "What her commitments are?" Hugh knew all of this but when laid out like this he truly understood and he shook his head yes.

"I knew, but I didn't realize" Hugh said.

"Hugh my boy, you are an awesome catch, If I were a nineteen year old girl in the market for a handsome, strong young man,

You'd be it" "But April is not there, not yet" the Judge said.

"I also believe April is one whale of a catch April is kind, caring, and exemplifies all the characteristics of a loving wife and Mother one day."

"She helps anyone who needs help weather they ask for it or not. April is not afraid of anything and at this rate, she might be President one day." and they both laughed.

"What I want you to know is this. April loves you as a person. She would be lost without your friendship. And if you are willing to be patient and wait, she will come to you when she is ready.

If you understand horses", Hugh nodded his head yes,

"April is like a filly, full of excitement, loves to run and play. But always comes to Momma when she needs comfort." "To tame a filly, you need to be in her life, around her. She gets used to seeing you and will come you. But do not put a rope around her, she will run. Just let her be."

"She will tease you, play with you and in time, she will slip her head under your arm and stay there. In time she will like you more than Momma and come to you for whatever reason." the Judge said.

Hugh added, "What about a stubborn filly?" The Judge said, "They're no different, they just take longer."

"They may need that confirmation, they must, must have it especially if they have abandonment issues. They are the strongest, independent creatures, and if you gain their trust you have won something that will never ever leave you and will protect you with her life."

Hugh understood, "I am glad we had this talk, I think the world of April and one day, one day, between you and me, I hope to marry her. She is all I want in a wife, life will never be boring" Hugh said.

"So I thought this trip was to have me change career choices, not to enter the military" Hugh said. The Judge started his truck and said, "Between you and me, I am proud as hell of you for your choice and commitment. I did it, so did April's father, it's your life and the military is good to find your resolve. What branch are you considering?" "The Marines I think" said Hugh. "I was in the air force and April's father was in the Army" the Judge said with a big smile.

"I did not talk you out of the military but I think you understand the precious gem you hold in your hand." The Judge said. "I do sir, and I am going to call April and apologize, and ask her to the movies. I am crazy about her and would never jeopardize doing anything to chase her away" Hugh said.

Down the hillside they came, bouncing all the way. Mrs. Marshall saw them and hoped the Judge was successful, She was heartbroken when she saw the Judge shrug his shoulders as if he failed, but he did not fail. This was path Hugh was on was corrected for every ones sake, everything happens for a reason.

That afternoon the telephone rang at the Di Angelo's home, it was 12:00 in the afternoon. "Hello" said Miranda, "Oh hello Hugh, just one minute". "April! April telephone", and she came into the kitchen quickly asking who was it?" Miranda simply handed her the phone. "Hi April, this is Hugh Marshall. There is a movie playing in town today, I was wondering if you would go with me I'd feel kind of funny going alone" April stood there unsure what to say, Miranda was at the end of the table nodding her head yes. "Ah, ok, yeah sure, I will go with you" said April. "Ok I will see you about 7:15 ok? The movie starts at 8 and I thought we could grab a bite to eat or an ice cream cone."

April smiled, "That sounds great, see you then." April told her Mom she had to get a start on the feeding or she would not be ready in time. So out the door she bounded, in a hurry as always. Miranda stood there hopeful. Maybe this will all come together after all.

It was the New Year and in Spring Hugh would graduate in June. He had a one year delay for entry into the Marines. He was entering the Marines.They had several dates that were fun. They went snow mobile riding and April took Hugh out on her kind of snowmobiling, on a horse and sleigh and Hugh really enjoyed that. He liked doing anything with her. They both worked in projects with the church for members and for their community.

During winter they and the young men and women built over One hundred snowmen lining the town. They were dressed complete with carrot noses and coal eyes. The people loved it. Many drove to the town to see all the snowmen. That was featured in the newspaper and of course on the radio.

Flo

Spring was coming on, the primaries for election and April & Miranda were asked to come to a flower social. It was hosted by one of the women on the city council. First came April's birthday. All she wanted was to eat out at Flo's restaurant.

Giving her Mom some time off and she missed seeing Flo and the gang. When they entered there was that familiar sound of the tinkling bell. "Well, well, look what the wind blew in" said Flo and she came around to hug April. "My you have grown. You are so pretty and strong. You have muscles in those arms" she commented.

As they sat down Flo came with menus and April asked where Amy was, she was always there. "Well Amy has had a streak of bad luck". She had a mammogram and they found a spot and then they did a biopsy. It was cancer. She is going in for a whack job, you know, and her hands went across her both breasts. "A double mastectomy?" asked Miranda. "Yes, that's it" said Flo "Like I said a real bad stroke of luck". Miranda and April looked at each other and both of their minds whirled.

April asked, "Would it be possible for me to work a shift here every day?" I mean I could work for Amy and give her the money. I don't want it." Gordon looked at his daughter, always wanting to help. Well I could take care of the ponies and….. Miranda interrupted him. "No, I will take care of the ponies, you feed the calves" and April can come and work from morning to afternoon. And I also think we need to have a prayer chain. Put her name on the prayer rolls in the temple.

It was planned at that dinner table at a delayed Birthday for April, it was a great gift. Right then they spoke with Flo who was taken aback that April would do this for Amy, and of course she welcomed April to work with them. So that weekend April began. "She earned $12.00 an hour plus tips. The tips outweighed the salary because of what she was planning to do. Some days she earned over three hundred dollars, sometimes more.

The cash was given to a very reliable source in an envelope who delivered it to Amy's home every week. It was just Amy and her husband, but Amy's salary paid for many things. The electric, telephone and many other expenses. Then one day Flo told April Amy's washer and drier went on the fritz, the repair man looked at it and he said it would cost too much to repair.

So April called Mr. Stevens, the manager of all the farms and asked him to make a purchase of a good washer and drier for the Princes. Hobens delivered a good set to the objection of Amy's husband. He said he could not pay for them and insisted the man take them back. It was quite a problem and the Sheriff was called. When Gordon saw what was going on, he sat Mr. Duane Prince down in his living room and talked with him. "Now Duane, you and Amy have lived her for over forty years. Everyone in town knows Amy. I think what happened here is a lot of love and care from your friends in the community.

They all want to help but don't know how. So let them Duane, please. Don't' make this job so hard for the Hobens man, it's not his doing. Duane was almost to the point of tears. Gordon asked if he could send in some additional help. Women to help clean, do laundry and cook, as Duane worked full time and Amy was struggling.

That is how the Relief Society was called and utilized for a family who were not members of their church but of their community well known and loved. Amy was weak, so the sisters had her drinking broth from the real deal, not a cube. They spoke with her, washed her, cleaned, cooked, and lifted both her and Duane.

And the money, where was the money coming from Amy asked. No one knew. It was put into the bank each week by one of the sisters. In time with good care, prompt visits to her Dr. and chemo, rest and encouragement, Amy healed, slowly but surely.

April enjoyed the diner. She met a lot of good people. She remembered some of them who were happy to see her again. They commented on her in the Olympics and racing. They were at the barbeque and had such a wonderful time it was like a community picnic they said. In time many teens began to come, many were class mates of April's, in the school.

They loved the rodeo burgers and many of the items on Flo's menu. The food was better tasting and the more social than fast food places. So on Friday nights it was nothing to have over two hundred people for a meal. Flo was overwhelmed but loving it.

April was busy. Flo had to hire another woman to help. Sometimes April waited tables, sometimes she washed dishes. She loaded the dish washer and sometimes she cooked. Yes she cooked.

On weekends April's parents would come in. The place was packed teenagers everywhere. Gordon and Miranda sat down. April came over dressed in her waitress uniform & hat. May I help you?" she asked, they all laughed including those in the diner at the time. Gordon looked around and suddenly everyone was eating or reading or looking very busy. That was the power of the Sheriff, he commanded respect. Her parents ordered and their food came out exactly as they liked it. "Did you cook this?" her Mother asked, and April curtsied and said, "Yes Mam I did" and Flo backed her up.

This job kept April busy from April until July. She was allowed off for Hugh's graduation in June and the flower social in July. But faithfully she did all she could at home and worked at the diner. Flo was talking to the Judge one day and asked about something that had not happened since he graduated

He said he was interested, but wanted to wait. She had two more years to go.

Hugh came into the diner often. He ordered an orange freeze or French fries.

He would watch April and talk to her when she had some free time. She was so kind and patient with the elderly people and little children. She never hurried them and made suggestions for them. She never needed a ride it was either Flo or another woman who worked there who lived out near April. Hugh found that trying to make time with April was difficult he had to "schedule" a date.

The best time to find her was very early in the morning after her chores, she was usually done and off for a run. She would catch up with a runner "The Captain who was retired from the U.S. Army. He was an amazing person, in great shape for his age. Those two made good running companions. They were serious and did not talk much. It was very hard to talk to April on a run.

But the walk back was awesome. April was all sweaty and mellow. He was able to pick her brain and make her laugh. Often Hugh took April's hand and swung it in extremes, back and forth which made her laugh. The thing that gripped Hugh was how easy it was to be with her. No pressure, mostly fun or getting things done. April never ordered. She asked. April was a natural athlete and a natural trouble maker for fun.

She would dot his face with ice cream cone she would splash him with water or mud whatever was handy. Yep, she was a stinker sometimes.

Hugh's Prom

Graduation was something Hugh wanted done and over with. He did not want to go to the prom. The girl he wanted to take could not go. She was working. But his Mom pressured Hugh to ask a girl, any girl. But he was not one to be pushed around. To keep his Mom from grumbling, he went, alone. He sat there for a while listening to the band. Some girls asked him to dance and he shook his head no. Twenty minutes of that and he walked out.

Hugh headed to the diner and there was his girl. She was dishing out some ice cream with whipped topping. He came in with his tux and sat on a stool. Some whistled at him he sat down.

"I'll have some of that" he said to April. She smiled at him which always melted his heart.

"Would you like one or two scoops, fruit or whipped cream" April asked.

"I want the works you pick the fruit and top it with the cream." April put on four scoops of ice cream, strawberries and whipped cream and brought it to Hugh.

Some of the customers commented, wanting what Hugh had. "It's not your prom" April said to them and they laughed. April sat on the empty stool beside Hugh tapped his hand and said, "Guess what?"

"Amy is coming back on Monday, isn't that great?"

"Really, she is all better?" Hugh asked.

"Her Dr. says so, she is clear, she is cleaning at home, and feels ready to come back. Not a full day but half a day to start."

"That's awesome" said Hugh. And he meant it. Cancer survival is something to celebrate.

"So soon I will be unemployed" April said.

"You can come back and work with us anytime, you're a hustler" Flo said from the back room who was listening in as usual.

Hugh put his arm around her and said, "You have done an amazing thing. Not everyone would volunteer to do this and you never complained.

"If I complained it would be better if I did not do it, the truth is I loved it."

Flo hollered out, "If you kids want to go, just go ahead and leave, I will close up"

April got up and got her purse and things. She spoke with Flo briefly and then wanted to use the telephone to call her Mom.

April wanted to let her know she was coming home with Hugh.

They left in Hugh's big pickup truck it was noisy because it was diesel. On the way home they saw some other kids from the Prom who beeped their horns to Hugh and he tooted back, he had a musical horn that sounded like "CHARGE"! it made April laugh.

In no time they were at April's home, the porch lights were on. Hugh got out and went to April's door and opened it for her.

April was impressed! No one ever did that for her. Hugh always did. He walked with her up the steps to their home and went inside with April.

Miranda was in the kitchen and was wide eyed when she saw Hugh, "Hugh you are so handsome in that tux."

Hugh got embarrassed and said nothing.

Gordon came out and shook Hugh's hand thanking him for bringing April home.

April told her parents the good news about Amy coming back. Miranda had her hands on her face surprised and relieved for Amy. Gordon called them into the parlor and said, "Come on in, it would be such a shame to waste that Tux Hugh. As they came in the music began to play.

Gordon took his wife's hand and began to pull her close to him and dance.

He looked at Hugh and said "Come on man, get a girl and dance" So Hugh smiled and pulled April to him.

Hugh was in his tux and April in her waitress uniform complete with stripped hat.

April reached up and pulled the hair pin out from the hat and it came off. Her curly hair tumbled down on her shoulders, and they danced.

Hugh held her close, not too close, and he thought this was the best time ever. Better than the prom. They danced to five songs and they all had enough. Miranda went into the kitchen and pulled out some fruit salad and some cake she had made hoping to see Hugh.

The cake was coconut cream, Hugh's favorite. Hugh was blown away he sat down and had both the fruit salad and cake that he thought was delicious. To say he was impressed was an understatement and it felt good. This is what he wanted for his own life, a wife to love and adore and to enjoy cake with friends. All Hugh wanted was a simple life.

Soon it was 10:00 p.m. past that magic hour that April had to go to bed, her day started earlier than most. Tomorrow she went back to her routine.

Hugh went to leave and Miranda thanked him for coming. Gordon shook his hand. April asked him to lean forward and she kissed his cheek and his face flushed red. "Good night" he said and he was in his truck in two steps.

As he pulled up into his driveway, Hugh did not remember how he got home. His mind was not on driving. He was still in that parlor room dancing with his girl. It was late, the kitchen light was on he knew his Mom was waiting up and would want details. He got out of his truck and hurried up the stairs walking into the kitchen. His mom was sitting there she was tired but he knew she waited to know. "How was it?" she asked. "It was amazing" Hugh said. "Really did you really have a good time?" Elaine asked. "I had an amazing time" Hugh answered.

Elaine was still curious, "Did you dance with any girls?" she asked. "I sure did" Hugh said, "A lot of them, it was really great." Elaine was satisfied, she yawned and said, "I am going to bed, please hang the tux so it is in decent shape when I return it, ok?" "Good night Hugh" and she left the room.

Hugh turned out the lights and went to the far end of their house his bedroom was downstairs ever since he and Trevor wanted separate bedrooms. He took off his tux and neatly hung it up on the shop hanger and went to take a hot shower. Hugh was soon in bed but could not sleep he laid there for a long time thinking.

How could he speed up time or slow it down. Hugh opted for a delayed entry to military school for one reason. Maybe it was a good thing, and maybe it wasn't. Either way, time would pass and he would find out. There was nothing he could do about it, nothing!

The Flower Show

The social elites of Fresno were all in a flurry, decorating the back foyer of the hotel. The courtyard and the pool area for the upcoming flower show. Mrs. Walker was almost red that everything was not at place. She was a short round woman with a fiery temper. She was always one to get things done, but this year she was not feeling herself. "Two days" people, "Only two more days and the show is here" she said frustrated. She had to go out and fan herself out side to cool off.

There were all sorts of flowers arriving, some from private residences and some from green houses that were all competing for the coveted green thumb award. April was asked if she would help carry in some of the decorations by one of the local flower shops. They were asked to do the decorating of the entire show so there were several vans coming and going bring in things, leaving to pick up more, everyone hustled.

There were sprays of flowers on over hangs as you entered, long ribbon drapes of crepe paper of all colors displayed for effects, it really was lovely. April could not name all the types flowers there were so many. Some had flowers, some did not. Some were plain and some dazzled with vibrant color and foliage. Every display was for sale. If you liked it all you had to do is mark the tag with your name and it was yours. You had to pay the price on the tag, and after the show take it home.

Mrs. Walker saw April as she sat there outside getting air. "How are you dear? Are you ready for the flower show? I mean do you have a song picked out?" April was prepared but the song she picked was simple and was not sure Mrs. Walker would approve of it. So she just said "Yes, I am ready."

The next two days flew by. Miranda bought dresses for the event for her and April. She made some changes on April's dress herself. April's dress was white with a yellow sash with flowers adoring the chest area. Puffed sleeves with lace on the ends. The hem was a string of flowers all of the embroidered flowers in the Hem bin at the local dime store that Miranda could find. Sunflowers, roses, multi mix and many more and when it was done the dress was beautiful.

They readied about 9:00 a.m. the social started at 10:00 a.m. with a luncheon at noon. Gordon was off and was able to do the feeding of the animals.

As the "girls" were ready to go Gordon whistled at them, "My oh my, look at the beautiful women who live in my house" he said. Miranda smiled and looked at him saying, "In your house? I believe you mean in OUR house. This house does not stay kept up by wishing Mister." Gordon crossed the room to kiss his wife and she protested saying "Don't mess my hair or make up, please?" He laughed at her, swatting her on her backside telling them to have a good time.

At the flower social Mrs. Walker was beside herself, the food was not ready. The chairs were not all set up. Her speakers were not there yet. She fanned herself constantly.

Soon the dignitaries came in white limousine's. April and her Mom were right behind them. Valets took the vehicles and parked them in the hotel's parking lot and would retrieve them as needed.

Mrs. Walker was so glad to see them come she took a few steps backward and almost fell. April was concerned and asked Mrs.

Walker to sit down and stay there. In the crowd were a couple of Doctors that April knew. She approached one of them and asked if they had any "tools" to check blood pressure. Dr. said she had a cuff and stethoscope in her car. April got a valet and asked him to bring them in to where Mrs. Walker was sitting.

The Doctor checked Mrs. Walker's blood pressure and it was up, way up! She advised Mrs. Walker to sit and stay sitting, for twenty more minutes and she would recheck it for her. "Oh my, I can't sit, I have this social to put on." April looked at her directly in her eyes and said "If you don't listen to the Doctor you might not be here at all. Why not let someone help you. I can read. I know many of the people and you relax." "Me? Relax? That is out of the question, I never am like that" she said. Then the Doctor replied, "If you don't relax soon there will be no more you."

This is serious and after this event I want you to go to county general. I will write a script for you for an EKG. I believe you should be on a blood pressure pill to manage the blood flow to lower your blood pressure. I will be at county general right after this event, so I will see you there?

"Ok, ok, I will" I just want to enjoy this event, I look forward to it every year" Mrs. Walker said. "Then let me help you" April told her. Mrs. Walker handed April "her" program.

The staff found a wheel chair for Mrs. Walker and with great protest she finally sat in it. You never knew she was in a wheel chair with her sitting behind the head table. She sat right beside the podium allowing her access to the microphone when needed. On went the show! Introductions were made by Mrs. Walker and some of the dignitaries were introduced. She then said the song would be by April Di Angelo followed by an invocation by Reverend McKay.

Thankfully someone made sure a piano was right near the front to the right side of the stage. April got up, went to the piano and began to play and sing: Whenever I hear the song of a bird, or look at the blue, blue sky Yes, I know Heavenly Father loves me." Then when she stopped she nodded at Reverend McKay to give the invocation.

April bowed her head until Reverend McKay was finished. She stood up to join her Mother and was greeted with a squeeze by Mrs. Marshall. "You did wonderful dear" she said to April. Who thanked her and sat down by her Mom. Miranda patted April's leg and smiled at her daughter.

Two seats over someone got their attention and asked about that song. Where did it come from? She loved it so much. April told her it was from their church. It was in their church's Children's hymn book. The woman wanted to know more. Well that is something April thought. She took the woman's name and number for future reference.

The judges had already made their pick, and everyone was welcome to listen to the seminar while the looked at the many flowers.

One of the staff came out and announced the lunch was ready. Mrs. Walker motioned for April to come forward.

"Will you make that announcement for me dear. I am not feeling so well she said. April looked at Mrs. Walker and her color was changing. She quickly notified the Doctor and had staff call an ambulance ASAP. Then they both wheeled Mrs. Walker out quietly while everyone was still looking at the many flowers. Mrs.

Walker was loaded into the ambulance, they put her on O2 and off they went.

"Geez Louise, I sure hope she is alright" April said. The Doctor standing there asked to be excused. She wanted to go and see how Mrs. Walker was, as well. It was not said, but April feared Mrs. Walker had had a heart attack.

The luncheon went on without a hitch, and everyone was pleased. They looked for Mrs. Walker. So April took the microphone and said Mrs. Walker had to leave suddenly. It was of family concerns, not to worry. She would be back if and when she could. No one suspected anything they all knew Mrs. Walker was raising her daughter's child, who was at times difficult to say the least.

After the luncheon the winner of the coveted green thumb award was given out, and the winner was so happy she cried.

April and her Mom were glad the event was over. They sought out the manager of the hotel asking if there was anything they could do since Mrs. Walker had to leave. So far as they knew, after the flowers were gone, all that was left was clean up.

April gathered up all Mrs. Walkers papers. She put them gently into her portfolio bag, it was like a suitcase. She told her Mom she was ready to go. They swung by Mrs. Walkers home and found her husband mowing grass. They told them what had happened and he took them into his home where the county general hospital did indeed call him. They left her bag with him and he went to shower and change to leave to see his wife.

Hugh's Graduation

The Di Angelo's were relieved Mrs. Walker was alright. She came home in two weeks, with care. They were also gearing up for Hugh's graduation from High School. Hugh did not want any fuss. But like it or not the Marshalls invited the Di Angelo's and they were all going. Hugh got several awards and everyone was so proud of him. He really was a good boy all through High School.

After the graduation, there were refreshments in the cafeteria and many families ended up in the hall ways, it was less crowded and cooler. That is where the Marshalls were with the Di Angelo's. There was much chatter between them and that is when Hugh told April he had a delayed entry into the Marines.

April asked why he did that but he did not answer her. Well he did but it was so not Hugh, saying he was getting a job.

April did not understand why, she let it go and talked to other seniors wishing the best of luck. Some of them were taking the pilot program with D farms, which thrilled April but she said nothing.

Farm Competition

That summer flew by. There was a filly April & Marty were beginning to train for racing. She had great looks and potential. She was a daughter of Native Son. They raced her lightly, preparing for bigger events later.

April's schedule was still grueling she was in bed sometimes as early as 8 p.m., no later than 9:30 p.m. April was up by 3 a.m. fed all the animals at various farms. She mixed feed for the dairy cows for Beth. Helped her milk from 4:30 a.m. till 7:30 a.m. left and worked at home or helping someone from 9 a.m. until 10:30 a.m. By this time she would be in school, but since there was no school she rode Native Son or did chores from 10 a.m. until 3:30 p.m. In the evenings April milked the cows alone and then turned them out into the field for the night. Set the milk machines to be washed. She cleaned the milk house and by 7 p.m. she was finished.

Some days her parents would drag her to the Bandit for an ice cream cone, but she sometimes fell asleep in their truck.

She truly did have long days. Before she started her junior year of High School a flier came around for all companies in dairy. Encouraging youth to sign up for farm competition. The youth would be chosen to work at three different farms or dairies. They would rotate every three months. They would be critiqued and then at the end, one would be chosen as the winner. There was a huge cash prize.

April liked this idea and wanted to enter it in her Junior

Senior Year. She would only be missing half a year of school and this competition would be considered educational.

April spoke to her Parents about this and they were concerned. April already had a lot on her plate. So they decided to sit down as a family, make plans and see how it would work out.

Grandpa

One evening for Family Home Evening each one of them came to the table with their ideas. There were some groans and lots of laughter they never took life too seriously.

Miranda thought it was important April continue to go to church and the youth meetings on Wednesday nights. April agreed. April reluctantly gave up the pony rides. There was always some young person wanting to take the kids out. They got paid hourly, which made them happy. Most of the profit was kept by Di Angelo's rightfully, as they bought the ponies.

They fed them and took care of them and the equipment.

April introduced the idea of how the other farms owned under D Farms were being operated. She could not see why the Adams farm could not be done the same way. There would have to be some improvements and changes. Mrs. Adams could stay, as could Beth. There would be five or so other's people and Beth could decide who that would be. Those lucky chosen would have their educations paid for. That milk would go into the co-op. Both her parents liked that idea, so they turned that over to April to handle with Mr. Stevens. They already liked the new overhang milk improvements.

When the Di Angelo's were finished with their Family Home Evening, they put their papers away. Ruby began to bark and run towards the kitchen door and back again. Miranda got up and went to the door and was having a conversation when Gordon got up to see who it was.

There was an older gentleman at the door he looked a little

uncomfortable standing there with a tan jacket over his left arm and a small brown suitcase in the other. His English was understandable, although a bit broken. He tried to explain to them who he was. He kept talking about a letter.

When suddenly a light came on in Miranda's head! She welcomed him in. He smiled and shook Gordon's hand. Miranda led him to the kitchen where April was almost finished putting her papers and to do lists away. April looked up and studied the man. He did the same to her. She walked over to him and looked more when he said, "My April" holding out his arms. April thru her arms around his waist and hugged him, beginning to cry saying, "Grandpa, Grandpa". It was a very emotional, exciting event. So much the older man staggered a bit and Gordon gave him a chair to sit down. The old man wiped his brow with the hanky in his pocket. Wiped his glasses and smiled. "I have come, I have to see, you know?"

The Di Angelo's were a bit speechless. Miranda who was always quick on her feet was first to say "Welcome, our home is your home, we are so glad you came". Gordon followed suit taking the man's suitcase to the back sewing room that had been used off and on. It was not cluttered. Gordon placed the suitcase on top of the sewing machine lid which served as a table quite well. The bed looked made up just fine the way it was. Soon Miranda joined him pushing him out of the room to go and talk, while she put the finishing touches in the room. Out in the kitchen the Grandpa and April were having a whale of a conversation.

They talked about all of the things she had done since coming with the Di Angelo's. She spoke about the ponies and everything!

The old man asked to see the horses. The old man's eyes danced with joy, he was clearly mesmerized. Gordon and April went out to the ponies and the old man seemed disappointed. April told him the race horse was not kept on their farm. But tomorrow they would take him to see Native Son. His eyes brightened and he smiled.

Back in the house and the old gentleman explained his trip out to California He said he made a big lie. "I was to be in Portugal, but I come here to see her" he said with a big smile.

"My wife, she no understand this little one means so much to me. She no feel the same way, says this one spoiled & lies".

"I say no, I think and think. I go to church and ask God what to do. I pray and pray and then her Momma comes to me with the news. I was so happy I could not believe it I wanted to run here."

He told them where he grew up. All about his life in Portugal and how he had an arranged marriage from birth by his wife's family who paid a dowry to marry their daughter.

To ensure she would not live in poverty as a woman and when he reached adult hood he honored that agreement. They came to America and made their lives. They were dairy famer's with a small herd. He also purchased the farm where April was born. For his son to operate, But then he became quiet and stopped talking. Instinctively April stood up and held onto his arm, "It's ok Grandpa, you could not take care of everything. You see, it has all worked out." He squeezed her arm and looked at her with tears in his eyes saying, "Yes, it has I see that now."

Miranda brought in homemade jelly filled doughnuts with glasses of milk and the older gentleman gladly took one and smiled thanking her. "What time you milk in the morning?" He asked April. April looked at her parents and Gordon nodded at her. "I milk at 4:30 a.m. Grandpa, why?" "I come with, I come with" he said.

Bed time came very early. The old man neatly folded his clothing, used the bathroom downstairs and went to bed. April bound into his room and he sat up. "Grandpa, we did not have prayers" she reminded him. "Ok, I come" he said. He walked out in the living room with his boxer shorts and t-shirt and glasses. "My kind of guy" said Gordon smiling. They all knelt down on the floor and a prayer was offered to close their Family Home Evening.

And to give great thanks for the family that had come so far to see April. Grandpa peeked at his Granddaughter. Her eyes were sealed tight, her lips pursed, she looked like an angel kneeling there.

He felt a lump in his throat rise as he often did when he thought she was lost. The long prayer ended and April kissed everyone goodnight, and they all clamored to bed.

Not sure who would have won the snoring contest. It might be Gordon, but Grandpa was close behind. It was a long night for Miranda who eventually got up and got her ear plugs.

The next morning Grandpa got up at 4:00 a.m. dressed and stood at the kitchen door. The light above the sink was on, but not one sound.

He pulled out a chair and sat there waiting. Soon there was a sound of an engine and sure enough there was his Granddaughter at the wheel of a strange truck.

She half ran up the sidewalk and steps, opened the door and saw him and waved for him to "let's go". He walked down the steps and sidewalk into the funny truck, "What's this?" he asked her. "It's a gator, doesn't go too fast but gets me where I need to go, it's quite rugged" and away they went. Not fast.

April was respectful of her Grandfather sitting there in the passenger seat. She did not want to frighten him. At the barn they both got out and the cows were ready in line to go into the parlor.

April went into the milk house and washed her hands. Then she turned on the equipment, entering the milking parlor with her Grandfather behind her. She showed him how to swing the boom for the milk machines and how to wash the cows and dry them. They did the work together, it was not strenuous, no bending down to put machines on like in stanchion milking. It was not long with two, and they were both home before 5:00 a.m. laughing and talking.

Miranda was getting breakfast together with scrapple, bacon, eggs, toast and orange juice, and a bowl of fruits. Gordon and the old man talked about the dairy how different it was when he milked.

How much more efficient it was and easier for the cows. Yes, he had been impressed. And how interesting that this was something she had chosen to do, it was in her blood, there was no other explanation.

Gordon had to agree, he told the old man this was not what he wanted for his daughter.

It was time consuming and the old man laughed. "Keeps nose to grindstone, never any trouble and makes money" the old man said. "Well you are certainly right there" but as a sheriff I do the same but I have my weekends off and do get away once in a while.

Miranda was quick to reprimand him, "You do work

weekends Mr. Di Angelo. I know so, and we go away because I ask you and ask you to. They all broke out in laughter.

April explained this was the set up at all the D Farms. It was expected to be designed all the same way. The parlor was built with two up climb ends where the cows would come in single file 4 at a time. (on each side) The utters would be washed and dried and the milk machines were on swing arms. Two on each side, pull and slide the milk machine to where you needed it. Put it on the cows utter and wait 5 to 8 minutes, take it off go to the next cow waiting. She would be clean and dry. After one rotation when the last cow in that line was finished, the group moved out and another 4 in (8) total came in again. This way with four workers on for a week and then the next four would be on for a week, they could trade days or milking's it was up to them.

April still wanted to exercise Native Son and felt if they all went over to the barn both objectives could be met.

They did go. Gordon left for work and Miranda drove while Grandpa sat in the back seat. At the farm April got out and went in to find Native Son lounging outside. She grabbed a lead line to bring him into the arena.

Her Grandfather was standing there assessing him as the horse was unknown to him. As she brought Native Son to him, the horse stood there smelling this man. There was something peculiar about him, something very good peculiar about him. The old man walked close to Native Son and began to rub down his side and legs. He felt his muscles his tendons and deep spots. These hands had been educated around horses. He understood and he knew what he was doing. His father had been the care taker and trainer of horses for the king of Portugal when he was a small boy.

"He one fine horse April" he said "Very fine", nodding his head in affirmative. "Would you like to ride him?" April asked him.

"Me? No, no" and he laughed. "I am not kidding, he is not wild and he will be gentle with you." The old man looked up and said, "Ok". Native Son was quickly brushed and tacked up and talked to by April, "Please, you better be a good boy. This is your Grandpa too you know, so please be gentle I know you know, so try" she begged him.

The horse nodded as if he understood and he stared at the old man closely from his left eye. They old man was tender and Native Son's eyes grew soft. They bought Native Son out and used a step up for the old man to get on.

He was a bit off balance at first, but once on, feet in the stirrups he began to take on a persona of a different man. A younger man from long ago he held his back straight, looked forward, and commanded Native Son to walk.

They went around the big arena, all alone by themselves. He asked for a walk and then a canter. Native Son did not pull to go fast. It was a nice romp around the ring. For him, he seemed to understand he was carrying precious cargo. Then after three times around they walked again and he was reined to the step up. "Oh April, you make me a happy man" he slapped the horse lovingly on the side of his neck. Native Sons ears went up to show his approval. "I get off now" and he carefully lifted his leg over the horse and stepped on the step up with some assistance not to fall. Native Son stood very still.

"He a great horse" "I so glad to come and see him and ride" with that he winked at April. Then one of the staff took Native Son back out untacked him to be turned out again. Before that

Grandpa had brought along an apple and offered it to the horse. Native Son took the apple with great gusto, loving it.

Grandpa laughed and laughed. "Oh I have so much fun, I love all this good life" he hugged his Granddaughter. They soon were back in the car to show him the town, and meet some of the people and have lunch.

They stopped at Flo's diner for a quick bite to eat and to acquaint Grandpa with some of the town folks. Gordon joined them and the four of them had a nice relaxing lunch.

A quick stop at the grocery store and they were back home in no time, Miranda had to get dinner started. Tonight they would have fish in honor of their guest with parsley tiny red potatoes, a salad and rolls. Grand pa began to roll up his sleeves to wash his hands and help. Miranda told him she wanted no help. She wanted him to visit with his Granddaughter that is what he had come for, so he did.

He walked around in the house seeing all the photos, some old, some of April's brothers that she had kept, some of her in the Olympics. Those were impressive. He looked at the case with the medals hanging inside and tears began to well in his eyes. She had come so far and had done so much with her life. She was truly brave, strong in heart, so much like he had been as a young man. Of all the children this is the one who reminded him of what he was like when he was young.

Like a bull, could do anything.

The rest of that day and the days following the old man made himself useful. He fixed things around the farm. He fixed broken boards, gates that did not close right.

He sawed, glued, wired, painted, welded, hammered, screwed,

nailed, he hung up things. He pulled wires, sledge hammered posts, cut grass with a scythe cycle, he made himself quite useful and good to have around. Yes it was a busy week they worked together, played together. While she worked with him, more and more memories crept back into her mind.

They took him to the ocean and out to eat, to the ice cream stand, and to a race that April entered a B race for fun. Can you guess who won? Yes, it was a wonderful ten days for him, all of them. He loved the unity of the family, he admired that they prayed together at meals and every night at bedtime, on their knees.

It made prayers really mean something more meaningful that way. He loved that she attended church every Sunday they all did as a family. Yes, he loved it all, and could see what had happened, what had gone wrong in his son's life and family.

It was not just a shame, it was a damn shame. A tragedy that never should have happened!

It was all because of laziness and complacency. They found other things to do on a Sunday instead of going to church. They missed out on going to church to secure unity of a family. God should be the center of a home and he was sure about that. He and his wife had not had an easy life.

They made it because they kept God in their life going to church. They kept Christianity in their home. They had made it to fifty six years of marriage. Sure it was not easy. They did not always agree, but they worked it out. That is what you are supposed to do. Man is to obey God, and the woman obeys man, not in a forceful way but in humility and in love.

The old man was happy, happier than he had been in years.

He had found her, the lost one. Her life was full and happy. He was regretful he had to lie to come. When he got home he would tell the truth to his wife, and remind her why he did lie to go.

One evening while mixing feed for the dairy cows as she always did, Grandpa sat on a chair watching her. He watched her calculate the amounts of each batch of silage, hay ledge, soybean and corn to be fed. He was proud of her, she was not yet Sixteen and could run a farm by herself. He knew she would be alright she could take care of herself.

He felt warm and wiped his brow and face. She came to him and said, "Grandpa, this is not the East. It is the west and you are dressed too warm." She unbuttoned his white shirt and had him take it off he was also wearing an undershirt. She hung his white shirt on the chair he was sitting on. "Much better" he said smiling.

As he sat there she came to sit with him, "Grandpa, I wish you did not have to go back, I wish you could stay here, we sure are thankful for your help. Is there anything you don't know how to do? She asked him. "I don't know how to leave without sadness" he answered her. She instinctively squeezed his hand and he squeezed hers back.

She told him as they had worked together on the farm she remembered working with him many times before. He nodded his head. "Yes, my April, you were with me many days, many times. Your Grandma no like you because you look like your Mother, crazy I know."

"She should not talk, she no look nice to anyone" and he smiled. April replied, "I have good and bad days, but each day I wake up I try to choose the better part, to be happy. I sing, I pray sometimes when I mix feed in here that makes me feel good inside. "Yes, its good" he said. Suddenly there was someone coming into the feed room.

Right where they were sitting! It was Manny, Miranda's father, April's other Grandfather. April's Grandfather stood up and looked at the dark skinned man. They both stared and then held out their hands to shake. Manny put his arm around the older man and hugged him.

"I am so happy to meet you, you must come and meet my wife and come to our home for a visit and you too as he hugged April." Manny took Grandpa, while April finished her job of mixing feed.

It was controlled chaos outside about eleven of Manny's family came along to meet Grandpa. They took him by surprise and he was a bit overwhelmed. Up on to the big porch and they talked and talked until late in the night. That night it was decided that Grandpa from the east would travel to Mexico to stay two days with Grandpa and Grandma from Mexico and April would be going along. Beth was more than happy to help and do the milking. it was much easier since revamped, and family is important, she said.

Grandpa had the time of his life. Never did he ever imagine he would travel to Mexico or be welcomed in by strangers who were family. It was a very pleasant surprise indeed. The meals were heavenly.

Everyone was busy, everyone was organized and helpful. It reminded him of when he was a young boy in the village. So many good times, so many good memories, and he wished his wife had been with him. It was his fault she was not.

But he just could not tell her the truth, it would have been argument after argument and he did not want that in his home. He loved a life of peace, and that is what he felt here with these strangers, who were now family.

The two days flew by he met Beauty and never would have guessed he had been so mean and wild. And the stories he heard about who broke him and how, it was amazing to him. He truly began to see how much this little one had grown, so much like his own people.

Those two days flew by and they were indeed wonderful days full of memories that Grandpa would enjoy evening after evening for many years to come. How fulfilling this trip had been. In the beginning he was worried and was deceitful to come. He left full of anticipation and he was so grateful he had come. So much he wanted his wife to come, to see for herself.

He had in his pocket pictures of this last ten days, as he packed his meager belonging into his suitcase and snapped it shut.

He surveyed the room to be sure he did not leave anything behind. A knock came on the door, he said, "Its' open" and April came in. She walked to him and hugged him around his waist. She looked up at him with tears in her eyes thanking him for coming and hoped he would come back.

She said "I love you Grandpa, I feel such a strong bond between us and I never want to lose that. I want to thank you for all you did for us here and for never giving up on me." "I just found you Grandpa, are you sure you don't want to move here to be with us?" she asked him.

"Oh my April" he sighed, "No my life is back there" and he pointed to the wall. "I will come again, I promise, I want to see you grow, be married and have little ones." and he tweaked her cheek. He felt her put something in his pocket, but did not move.

Gordon was standing to leave for work and was going to drop Grandpa at the bus station. He felt it was best for the women to stay behind. It would make it easier on April, and Grandpa was in complete agreement with him.

Miranda handed Grandpa a bag and said to have it on the bus. It was a meal and then some. "I take bus to airport" and eat it in airport" he said and thanked her.

He turned once more to see his Granddaughter standing there, he touched his chest with his fist and said, "You make me proud, be good girl, and make me prouder" he hugged her briefly and they left.

April was so confused, she remembered him. He was definitely there in her memories. More so than anyone else and with him coming the memories increased. He used to swing her on a homemade wooden swing, so high her feet would touch the tree boughs. She would giggle so much her tummy would hurt. "Oh Grandpa, Grandpa, my belly hurts, this so fun." She remembered him in a barn, calling to her as he squirted milk into a cat's mouth from a cow's teat. She remembered planting flowers with him, moving pigs, falling in mud, going fishing from the side bank of a creek side, with him wearing a silly floppy cap with fish fly ties on it. Yes, she remembered him so deeply in her heart it hurt. She prayed that she would not lose him. Not yet, Please Dear God, protect him and watch over him, keep him safe. Let us reunite again and have joy with each other's company. She repeated this prayer in many different ways, so many times, over many, many nights.

Back home after the Portugal trip, he confessed the truth

to his wife of sixty-five years. She was not surprised in fact she suspected it. He showed her the pictures.

He told her of how he rode the great horse, like in the newspapers. It was all true, it was her. She rode like the wind she skied down ice with grace of angels at her side. He told her things that even she marveled at. He showed her pictures of her medals.

"She no have big head", he said, "Not proud, not haughty, she is a nice girl, strong, work hard, likes milking Momma. She likes milking cows" and he laughed and laughed dancing around in a small circle.

She was glad he had gone. She knew the toll of this one missing had on her husband. She did not know why it struck him so hard but it had. She could not argue about this, she had not seen him this happy in a long, long time. So it was not a trip to Portugal, but the difference between Portugal and California was the point. He had found something very important to him in California he already knew what was in Portugal.

One morning as he dressed for church the old man smoothed out his pocket and felt something strange. He put his hand inside and pulled out a ribbon, and on the very end was a red horse, a bright red horse that looked like the race horse he had rode on. She had put it there, for him, it was a treasure indeed. He put it back in this pocket and patted it and sighed.

And for them all life went on. That hum, that stride that keeps you moving forward. You can always look behind you and see where you were, what you did and who you were with. Happy or not, but we all walk forward, one foot after the other.

The Milking Schedule

APRIL FELT THAT IF SHE RAN SHE WOULD ONLY BE ABLE TO SERVE 2 years, then she had to leave for the farm competition. So someone would have to stand in 1 year in her absence. "Do you mean you would be gone from the end of September to the following September, for one whole year gone?" Miranda asked. "Yes, that is how the brochure reads, they are allowed to call on Christmas Day and Easter, and if in the time frame on their Birthdays" Gordon said.

April looked at them both, "I don't need to do it, but it sounds interesting and would be great for D Farms. They money would help too. It's for a chunk of money that would help D Farms.

I believe that this next spring the filly will race and hoping she has a shot at the Triple Crown, even if she does go the distance that is June. I would not be leaving until late September.

"Mom, it is June, I have this summer and the entire school year and the next summer to be here. Then I would leave and be gone September to September, finish up eight more months of school and graduate" April said.

"Yes, I know but you always disappear on us, and we love you so much." Miranda said as she went to her daughter and held her close. April was smiling and her Dad winked at her.

So the farm was renovated and the barn extended. More cows were brought in 120 more, to make 300 cows to be milked twice a day. The 4 lucky people were chosen by Beth from a lottery list held by Mr. Stevens. Beth chose a girl from a town nearby, another girl from New York here to go to school, a boy from south California, and a boy from Nevada all four of them met a specific criteria. 1. All were from a broken home, either no father or mother. 2. serious about an education with no funds to pay for one. 3. Committed to stay, 4. Honest, chaste, decent and clean who loved their family. So as they came, they signed papers and found a room decorated it as their own and they took turns with different jobs but all of them milked. And it worked out well, so well that Beth was amazed.

Sometimes April would come and help out a bit, it was fun to get to know the new people and she liked milking cows some of the cows were quite personable.

The Accident

It was July when the sirens in Fresno went off on one afternoon. There had been an explosion at one of the plants. There would be professionals brought in but Gordon and his deputies responded as the events unfolded. The explosion was at large welding shop they welded large hulls for ships and box cars for trains. They employed over eighty employees and were busy all the time.

It was common for famers to take work to them for their equipment to weld. Tractors or frames it did not matter they did all sort of welding jobs. After looking around at the damage, it was found only one worker was injured but it was serious.

Dean Cramer was working up high, welding rivets into a side of a ship hull when the explosion occurred. He fell twenty five feet to the cement floor and when he fell the fear caused a heart attack. By the time the ambulance came, Dean was ashen colored, unresponsive.

The cause of the fire was determined to be a fuel line crossed with someone using an arc welder that never should have happened. The worker was new and did not know the layout of the shop.

He had been instructed to stay in one area and finish welding the frame of a cultivator that had cracked.

He had questions about another piece of equipment and dragged his line with him. Inexperience almost cost a man his life and did cause extensive damage to the business.

Dean was well known. He was a jovial man he loved to go fishing and he adored his two daughters Natalie and Megan. He often lovingly called them Nut-meg, his favorite spice. Dean's two daughters came regularly to ride ponies.

They lived in town and could not keep a pony there with them. They did not have enough income to board one either.

Dean's wife Reba was a stay at home Mom. She kept a neat home. Made good home cooked meals. Had a nice garden, and loved to sew. Where Dean was, so was Reba and the girls, they were a close family.

This news hit Fresno hard. Dean was the only income to his family and now he was at County Hospital fighting for his life. Gordon went in to see how he was the nurses told him little. Dean sustained the fall and the heart attack was bad. Dean was put on IV's meds, O2, as they were trying to manage him until he could go for surgery. By 5:00 the time he would be leaving his shift, Dean entered into the surgery center to repair his heart. Reba was at the hospital alone. It took a bit of calling but within an hour there were other women sitting with her.

Another took her daughters in her own home to play with her sons and have dinner and stay with them until Reba could manage.

This rocked April to her core. How fleeting life really can be. She felt she had to help. She had a friend drive her to the shop and she climbed the metal stairway to the office door. She knocked and the secretary was at the front desk. "Hello Cindy" she said,

"Is the boss in?" "Yes, he is April, just a minute." Cindy rang the intercom to let Mr. Hanson know April was there. Mr. Hanson opened the door and said, "Come on in April what may I do for you?" April carefully closed the wood and glass door behind her and sat down. "It's more of what I can do for you" she said. He looked at April curiously and asked her "Whatever do you mean?" April answered him. "What I mean is you just lost a great welder, who is going to be out for six months." Mr. Hanson wiped his brow and the room was not hot or humid. "I know, it was a terrible accident. He has coverage medically. All of his bills will be paid for thru our insurance. He does have work compensation, but of course it is not the same amount he earned.

April said, "I am offering myself, to work in his stead. Look Mr. Hanson I am a pretty good welder myself. I weld all of the machinery on our farm.

On the metal carts and Dad says I do a great job. It was Dean who taught me patiently. I tried it over and over with him until I got the hang of it. I am willing to work his shift on his jobs and you pay him weekly, not me"

Mr. Hanson looked at April incredibly, he was shaken. "April I can't hire you, you are not certified." "Oh you are mistaken sir, I most certainly am" April said. Mr. Hanson sat there for a minute then he said.

"How would you work the shift work, you go to school, don't you?" "I can work it out with the school so long as I know the shift." "I mean can't you help me out a little since my goal is to help him?"

"Oh yes, yes, I can" he said rubbing his chin, "And you say you don't want paid?" "Yes, that's right I don't want paid, but you will pay Dean his regular paycheck every week or two weeks. And you may not breathe a word of our conversation to him or anyone else. "Now April, if I hire you, you know darn well guys will see you on the floor and they will talk." Mr. Hanson said.

"Then it is your responsibility to talk to them before I start. It is none of their bee's wax what I do here" she said.

"Yes, yes, I suppose I should do that. So when do you think you would start?" he asked her. "I can start on Monday"

April said, I will come for day shift as Dean was on. But when school starts I will have to work the afternoon into evening shift" she said. "Well, how about coming in on Tuesday, I need to address all the men of this shop before you start" he said.

And that is how April began to Weld at the busiest weld shop in the area. She wore long sleeve shirts and pants and steel tip shoes. She riveted, she welded seams. April repaired parts and most of all she listened. It was not such a bad job, it was dirty, it was smelly but every place has dirt and smells.

It is what it is, April thought to herself. She put forth a good attitude making the best of things. Her Mom often made trays of cookies or sweet things for the guys. No man in the shop talked bad of her. They were impressed someone so young would care so much. She put her efforts into what she said. They treated her like one of them.

At a lunch or break time, if she did not come down, they would get her down. If her helmet visor was cracked they made her get another one. When she was there, she belonged to all of them they took good care of her. Oh sure she had the occasional cuts or burns, that was expected. They never saw anything like it in their lives.

For the three months it was easy, it was summer time.

She had time to go on some dates with Hugh and Wednesday Mutual nights. She rode Native Son and worked with that filly. She had a lot of free time. When school started that all changed.

She went to school from 8 a.m. to 2 p.m. Left and went to "work" from 3 p.m. to 11 p.m. On break time she did her homework, and at 11 p.m. she went home dog tired she would shower and go to bed. Often she was too tired to eat.

Miranda would cry, she knew April's hands were bad but she said nothing to anyone. The stress she was under is what caused her hands to break out. They were raw, bloody and pealing. Too often April forgot to take her medication with her. So she had to deal with it.

From June to October the months went by so fast. On weekends she spent her time with her Mom and Dad. She went to auctions to buy or sell. She bailed hay and helped where she could.

In October Dean was to be released for work. Nothing heavy, so Mr. Hanson decided to put Dean on sorting. The man who did this job was going to retire in January. It would give Dean three months to learn the job. It entailed sorting the metal bins, with a lift. No more lifting or climbing for Dean.

When the checks began to come in Dean's wife Reba called the office to speak to Cindy to find out what was going on. She did not want to get into trouble receiving workman's compensation and a paycheck.

Cindy said she did not know. If the checks were sent out, it must be right as everything was computer automated.

By January the truth came out, it happened quite innocently. Many of Dean's friends had come over and were drinking beer in the garage. Someone joked about having April come out and cover for them when they had their hang nail surgery and they all laughed.

Dean asked, "Why would you say something so dumb?"

"April was a nice kid, a decent girl." The group of them hung their heads and Dean pushed for an answer. When it came out, Dean was flabbergasted. Never in his wildest dreams did he think anyone would work in his job for him. Especially, not a nice girl like April. He went into his house to talk to Reba, he called to her and the two of them were in disbelief. That is when one of the guys came in and sat down at their kitchen table and told them what had happened. He made it clear no one was to say one word, not ever. He said

"The paychecks to you were important to her, but even more important was to keep this quiet. No one was to know, she wanted it that way. So let it lie, and keep it to yourself who knows in time she may need help too someday."

Fixing Up The Park

The elections were looming. The city park was in bad need of repair. So April organized a plan, everyone would purchase a brick, 1 red brick for five dollars at the park entry.

The charge on the wall was ten dollars, and twenty dollars to be at the fountain. The money raised would pay for the repairs. And every brick would have that person's name or the families name engraved into it. She went to the local brick yard and they let her have all she wanted.

The orders came in the mail along with cash and checks April knew many of the people who wanted a brick. The orders came in slow at first, and then Miranda had it announced on the radio every hour as a cute commercial. Then the orders poured in. They went to the city hall clerk's office she was a bit overwhelmed with the amount of mail that she received for bricks.

Some town folk, retired engineers came out to make the designs and when it was all finished the town park was beautiful. More people came to see it than ever before.

They all wanted to find their brick with their name or family name on it. This was a success in every way. The city park was beautiful complete with a fountain, scrolled railing, bicycle rails, a dog area, and last of all a lovers lane. Many people walked thru for exercise or to enjoy the out of doors.

This all came about without any tax increase or bill from the city. The citizens paid for the entire renovation of the park.

Many of the town men, women and children donated their time and talents. They could boast and feel proud that they helped turn their down town into a picture of beauty, because they really did.

The Election For Mayor

THE ELECTIONS CAME AROUND IN NOVEMBER APRIL COULD NOT vote she was not eligible because of her age. It was a heavy turn out with voters. By late night the election results were in the Mayor had 808 votes and April ended up with 1829 votes, the people had spoken.

At the acceptance speech April thanked the Mayor for his past service and promised to follow through on some of his ideas. She also promised the people to serve them. To do what was best for them and their town. In no way would she leave one leaf unturned in getting a needed project finished, and the crowd erupted.

So that is how a very young, mature, service minded young woman earned the respect of her community. By telling the truth and putting her values to the test. With each challenge she never bowed down and felt beat, yes it was close some times. And not always easy, but she tried, always tried to live the way the Savior taught by example.

Printed in the United States
by Baker & Taylor Publisher Services